EENIE MEENIE

WILLOW ROSE

Published by Jan Sigetty Boeje

Cover design by Jan Sigetty Boeje
https://www.facebook.com/pages/Sigettys Cover Design

Special thanks to my editors Jean Pacillo
http://www.ebookeditingpro.com

and editor Janell Parque
http://janellparque.blogspot.com/

To be the first to hear about new releases and bargains —from Willow Rose—sign up below to be on the VIP List. (I promise not to share your email with anyone else, and I won't clutter your inbox.)

- SIGN UP TO BE ON THE VIP LIST HERE :
http://eepurl.com/wcGej

Connect with Willow Rose:

willow-rose.net

I

"EENIE, MEENIE, MINY, MOE. Catch a *naughty boy* by the toe. If he screams *don't* let him go. Eenie, meenie, miny, moe."

The man was counting, pointing at the doors as he whispered the song in the dark hallway. His finger ended at door number nine. The man grinned and braced himself for what was ahead. He closed his eyes and took in a deep breath. It was important not to rush these things. It had to be done just right. He pulled down the ski mask to cover his face, then walked to the thick door and peeked in through the small window to make sure the boy was asleep. Then the man pulled out the keys and put one in the lock.

The boy was asleep in his bed when the man entered quietly. He didn't wake up even when the keys jangled in the lock. Not until the man was inside and had closed the door behind him, did the boy react. With a small shriek, he sat up.

"Who's there?" he asked. "Who are you? What are you doing in my cell?"

The man chuckled, but didn't answer. He walked closer while hushing the boy, as if he were a small child wakening from a bad dream, instead of a juvenile criminal facing his real punishment for what he had done.

"Hey. I asked you something," he said and got up from the bed. The boy was no more than fifteen, but working out along with the other prisoners had given him a muscular upper body that was very unusual for his age. His attitude suited his posture very well. He puffed himself up in front of the masked man and lifted his fists to show him that he would defend himself if the man came any closer. That didn't scare the man, though. He was prepared for him to try and fight back. They all did. But the man was ready. He pulled a stun gun from his pocket and walked towards the boy. The boy gasped and drew backwards against the wall. The man walked closer with the gun crackling in his hand, and as soon as it touched the boy and his body was shaking in spasms, the man knew it wouldn't take long before the boy would be like a puppy in his hands. Or maybe even more like a doll that he could do with as he pleased.

The man chuckled while the electric impulses ran through the boy's body, and as soon as he saw his eyes roll back into his head, he turned it off and let the boy's body fall lifelessly onto the bed.

"Time to get to work," the man said, and put his briefcase on the bed next to the boy. He opened it and looked at the tools inside. He picked up a pair of pliers and examined them, moved them a little to see if that was what he wanted to use. He looked at the boy. A third time offender. His first offense was stealing cars with his older brother. Second time he robbed a small store and beat the crap out of the owner. Third offense was what really ticked the man off. The boy and his three brothers had gang-raped a girl in an alley after a party. They spotted her at the party in a private home, and then followed her when she was walking home with her boyfriend. According to the boy's file they attacked the boyfriend from behind and beat him senseless with baseball bats, and then forced him to watch as they gang-raped his girlfriend.

That was what troubled the man. It's one thing to steal a car or rob a store to get cash. It was wrong, yes, and should be punished. But raping a fourteen-year-old girl and forcing her boyfriend to watch? That was too much. And, apparently, more than what the justice system could handle. The boy was more than they could cope with. One year in juvenile detention was the boy's sentence. Which would probably be reduced to six months if he behaved. The man felt his fury rise just thinking about it. In a few months, this boy would be out on the streets again, raping more innocent girls, beating more people up. And who knows what he might do next? The man knew these boys. They came back again and again. They never learned and the punishment the court gave them simply wasn't enough for them to stay out of trouble. And while they were inside the juvenile center? Well they just made new friends that were bad for them, who got them into more trouble as soon as they got out. It was a joke, really, the man thought. That was why he decided to take matters into his own hands.

The man looked at the tools and decided on the folding utility knife.

2

IT WAS JOHNNY'S FIRST time in the juvenile prison in Roedvig Stevns on the east coast of Zeeland. But it wasn't his first time in prison. He had done time before. Three times before, to be accurate, so it wasn't an unfamiliar situation for him to be put in the small cell with nothing but a hard bench to sleep on, a desk, a closet, a small fourteen-inch TV, and a sink.

"Here you go," the warden said, and Johnny stepped inside without a word. The door was closed behind him and locked.

Johnny sighed and sat on the bench. It was just as hard as it had been in the other places he had been. The barred window under the ceiling seemed smaller and the walls were all painted screaming yellow, those were about the only things that weren't exactly the same as in the other places. The other inmates probably would be too. It usually didn't take Johnny long to piss some of them off and get beaten up in the toilet-room. But he didn't care. He had gotten stronger while he was on the outside by working out a lot. Plus, he was older now and probably among the oldest. His experience would give him an advantage.

It hadn't been his plan to be in this situation again. After his third time on the inside, he decided it was time to change his life. Once released from the previous prison, Johnny hadn't gone back to his old friends. He moved to get away from them and to start a new life. Where it went wrong along the way, he now had two years to think about.

Johnny rubbed his forehead and stared at the window. He could see nothing but the sky from here. How he already missed the big outside. He sighed and hit a fist into the pillow.

"Damn you, Christian!" he yelled.

Christian was his younger brother. He was the reason why Johnny had ended up in here, locked up once again. Johnny picked up the remote to take his mind off his brother. The small TV under the ceiling made a noise and some news anchor started talking. Johnny wasn't in the mood for too much reality, so he flipped the channels and found an old re-run of *Friends*, one he had seen many times before, but still made him forget about his situation for just a few minutes.

As soon as it was done, Johnny's thoughts circled back again on his brother. Johnny didn't know where he was hiding, but he hoped it was a good place, since the cops were still searching for him. Johnny hadn't cracked. He hadn't ratted his brother out and never regretted not doing so. Johnny had told them he did it, that he had done everything, and no one else was involved. But, of course, they hadn't believed him. They threatened him with hell on earth if he didn't speak. They told him that they knew he was only taking the blame for his brother, and that all he had to do was to tell them that Christian was the one who had done it, and where he was, and then they would let Johnny go.

Of course, Johnny hadn't listened to them. Who listens to cops? Who would rat out his own brother? No, he'd rather serve time, even though he hadn't done anything. Even though he had finally gotten his life back on track. It didn't matter.

When it comes to family, you stick up for one another. You do what's necessary to help each other. Even if it means doing time for something you didn't do. It was beside the point.

Yet, they were still looking for him. They would be until they found him, they told Johnny. "We'll get him, and then we'll make both of you do the time."

Johnny had shrugged like he didn't care, but that was a lie. He did care. A lot even. Not about his own life. But about his brother's. Enough to take the fall. Doing time would have killed him. Christian wouldn't have been able to cope with it. Johnny had done it before. He could do it again. No problem. Anything for your brother, right? Even though he had been so stupid it made Johnny want to beat the crap out of him if he ever saw him again. It didn't matter.

There wasn't much Johnny believed in, but he did believe in family and the bond between them. He would die for his brother; even take a bullet for him right here and now if necessary.

And he knew that one of these days, it might just be what he had to do.

3

BRIAN WOKE UP TO the sound of screaming. He gasped and opened his eyes. It sounded like it came from the cell right next to him. Brian sat up and listened. The screams were spine-chilling. He breathed heavily. Anxiety took a hold of him. What could that sound be? What had happened to Ali in the cell next to his?

There was a lot of turmoil going on in the hallway outside, and Brian got up to try and look out of the small window, but all he could see were the tops of the prison guards' heads. He heard voices, some of them seemed urgent, but couldn't discern what they were saying. The screaming hadn't stopped; it continued on and on and left Brian terrified. Had someone hurt Ali in the middle of the night?

He ran to the window facing outside and tried to look down. He spotted blue lights and heard sirens in the distance coming closer. A few minutes later, he heard more voices outside his door. He ran back and peeked out. Now he saw some new heads, new faces. Paramedics, he thought. He watched as they carried Ali out on a stretcher. His body was covered with a white blanket, but it was already soaked in blood. Brian gasped and pulled away from the door. The guards soon knocked on all the doors and told them to go back to sleep. But Brian didn't sleep any more that night. He sat on the bed, waiting for morning to come, shaking in fear. This wasn't the first night he had been woken by the sounds of screaming. It happened a lot lately, but never so close to him, never someone he knew. Rumors flew around the inmates about who was getting hurt, but no one knew by whom or why. None of the guards seemed to care; they just shipped the injured off to the hospital and that was that. None of their business. Brian heard his own teeth chatter in the night. He was cold, but that wasn't what caused his teeth to rattle.

Brian stayed awake till the guards let him out for breakfast. His friends Gunnar and Torben sat with him at the table. No one said a word until Brian opened his mouth.

"Any news on what happened?" he asked.

Gunnar looked down, and then to each side, to make sure no one was listening in on their conversation. "They say he was castrated," he said.

Brian almost choked on his oatmeal. "What did you say?"

"You heard me," Gunnar said. "They cut off his dick, man. With a small knife to make it take longer and hurt more. At least that's what they say."

Brian lost his appetite. He pushed his bowl away. Torben took his and ate it like he was in a hurry.

"That's the second one this month," Brian said. "The second inmate sent to the hospital. What the hell is going on here?"

Torben was slurping as he gulped down the rest of Brian's breakfast. Gunnar sighed. He looked behind him before he spoke. "I tell you, something is wrong in this place."

Torben grunted and nodded while licking the spoon.

"I know," Brian said. "It's creepy."

Torben and Gunnar stopped eating and stared at Brian.

"What?" he said. "It's not like I'm scared or anything. I'm just saying it's real creepy, right?"

"Sure," Gunnar said. "But I know what I'm gonna do if they come into my room. No one messes with me. I'm gonna give them what they deserve. Ain't nobody gonna touch my dick, if you know what I mean."

They all nodded. Brian felt certain he could defend himself if it really came down to it. Lord knows, he had been through many fights and he always ended on top. Only sixteen, Brian was as tough as they get. But what worried him in this moment was that so was Ali.

Gunnar pulled Brian's sleeve. He nodded to his left. Brian looked in that direction and saw a guy, older than them by a year or two, a tough one, with a scar on his neck. Brian recognized the knife wound as he walked past them holding his breakfast tray.

"Who's the new guy?" Torben asked.

Gunnar bit the bread and pulled off a lump.

"That's what we're gonna find out," Brian said, while Gunnar chewed the bread with his mouth open.

4

JOHNNY SAW THEM FROM far away. He deliberately walked past their table so they could check him out. He knew they were the bunch he needed to hang out with in order to stay safe. They were the tough group, the ones who were in control. He could tell by the way they looked at him, the way they talked and comported themselves. It was the same everywhere. On the first day, it was all about making the right friends and the right enemies. Johnny was good at reading people. It had become one of his most cherished survival skills.

He gave the boys a look as he walked by, to show he wasn't afraid of them; he was tougher than they were and he would make them sense his strength, sniff him out if you'd like, like dogs did. Johnny knew they were gonna ask other inmates questions about him in the coming hours. They would have their little group of wannabes, reservoir dogs, to get them the information they needed on the "new guy."

Johnny sat in a solitary spot, feeling their eyes on his back and on his eagle tattoo that stared back at them. He wanted to show them he wasn't afraid to turn his back on them, he wasn't afraid to sit alone, he wasn't afraid of nothing. That would pique their curiosity, just like he wanted it to. As soon as they knew about him and what he was in for, they would come; they would approach him, and he would soon be part of their pack. It was all a game really, and Johnny knew exactly how to play it.

It didn't take long. In the afternoon when they were all sent outside to the courtyard, all three of them walked towards him. Johnny was sitting on a bench, smoking his third cigarette in a row when he heard their footsteps. He didn't turn around to look at them, but played it cool and kept his back turned to them until someone spoke.

"Hey, new guy," one of them said.

Johnny took a deep drag of the cigarette and blew out the smoke with a sigh. He turned his head and looked at them. He almost laughed when he realized how puny they really were. Three guys no more than sixteen, with their hands in their pockets, pants hanging by their knees. One of them wore a baseball cap and completed the picture of a boy-band gone wrong.

Johnny nodded with a grin. "What's up?" he said.

"We wanna talk to you," the one on the right said.

He was the stupid one. Johnny could tell by the look on his face. The follower. He was going to do anything Johnny told him to as soon as this little charade was over. The one in the middle was the leader. He seemed smart, Johnny could tell by his eyes; plus, he had the others do the talking. The one on the left was the tough guy. He spat on the ground and talked with the cigarette clinging to his lip in the corner of his mouth.

"What can I do for you?" Johnny said.

"Don't try and sound smart," the stupid one on the right said. "We do the talking."

Johnny repressed a chuckle and shook his head. "I don't think so," he said, and turned away from them again. It was all a fight for power from now on, and he had to show them he didn't bow to anyone.

Johnny didn't see it, but sensed what was going on behind his back. The small, feisty, tough guy stepped forward and wanted to start a fight, but the smart one stopped him, held him back. If he was as smart as Johnny thought, he knew they might be able to use Johnny; he would be good to have on their side. Apparently, he was. He walked around the bench and sat down next to Johnny. The two hotspurs stayed behind them.

"So, you're Johnny the Vampire?" he asked.

Johnny nodded, taking another drag of his cigarette. Vampire was the nickname he had been given after he bit a man and ripped off some flesh from his throat during a fight. It wasn't a nickname Johnny was sad about, but he thought it was a little overboard. All he had done was defend himself with all he had as a thirteen-year-old kid when his father attacked his baby brother with a knife.

Johnny spat on the ground and nodded.

"And you are?" he asked, looking at the guy next to him with the pretty eyelashes and very blue eyes.

"Brian."

"Nice to meet you, pretty boy Brian," he said and stuck out his hand. Brian smiled, took his hand, and shook it.

5

BRIAN WAS CONCERNED. Even though he had a new ally, a new friend who was extremely good to have on his side, he wasn't sure it was quite enough. No one knew who was behind the night attacks, but one thing was certain; it was someone with good connections and enough money to pay off the guards to let them in while the inmates were sleeping.

Ali had many enemies, especially in the West wing and, without a doubt, it was one of the guys from over there that had done this to him last night. It had to be someone he pissed off, Brian thought to himself, staring out the window of the prison church during the ceremony Sunday morning. They were all present. They had to be. All one hundred and twenty-four inmates in this juvenile prison had to go to the service on Sunday mornings. Those were the rules. Brian never understood why the prison forced them to go; none of the inmates listened to what the priest said. It wasn't like any of them was about to lay his life down to God and stop being who he was. Who were they kidding with this anyway? No one here wanted to repent. They all knew that God couldn't stand them for who they were, and he never would. Why else would he have given them such crappy lives? Why else would he have given Brian a father who ran away when Brian was only five and never came back? Why else would he have given Brian a stepdad who locked Brian in the bathroom so he could do nothing but listen when he beat Brian's mother? Why else would he have taken Brian's younger sister so early that she barely made it to be seven years old? Why would he let the stepdad beat her till she didn't move anymore? Why? Why would he let the stepdad get away with it, get away with telling the police it was Brian? Why would he let his mother be so afraid of the stepdad that she would tell the police the same, just because he was only eleven and too young to be punished? Why would he let them get away with it? Why did he let Brian live the next three years in an institution where he was exposed to drugs?

If God loved him as much as the priest claimed, then why did he let all those things happen? No, Brian figured all this out a long time ago. God didn't love him. He liked to see him suffer. God had deliberately given him a shitty life so he could sit up there and laugh at him as he struggled through it.

But Brian wasn't mad at God anymore, neither was he sad that he'd ended up in this place. For the first time in many years, he had a feeling of satisfaction. He got his revenge, not with God's help, but by his own hand. He still enjoyed thinking about the day when he tracked down his stepdad and attacked him with the knife. He remembered the sound of the knife going through his flesh. Every now and then, he could still feel the warm blood on his hands as it ran across them. He remembered the look in his stepdad's eyes when he pulled out the knife and stabbed him again, in the heart this time. Sometimes he even imagined it in slow-motion, just to get all the details right. The tip of the knife disappearing into his abdomen, slicing through clothes and flesh, right into his liver.

Then stab number two in the chest, ripping up veins and cutting through organs. Brian stabbed him ten times before he finally stopped. He even recalled the screams from people on the street, and the distant sirens when the police arrived and took him away. He spat at the dead body right before they pulled him to the car. Brian's hands were covered in blood, his nostrils filled with the sweet, red smell of revenge.

"Amen," the priest said and ended his sermon.

Brian looked up at the big cross behind him. The priest told them that he would be in the confessional if anyone wished to talk. Then he left. Brian sat still for a few seconds and watched as everybody got up and started walking towards the exit. Brian didn't move. He stared at the cross. It wasn't a Catholic church, but the priest put up a confessional anyway, just for them to be able to talk anonymously with someone, in case they needed to confess anything or just talk. A lot of the inmates did it just to lighten their hearts and get stuff off their chests.

Brian never considered the offer before, but now he did.

❧ 6 ❧

"EENIE, MEENIE, MINY, MOE..." The man was counting again. His finger ended on door number thirteen. As always, the man peeked in through the small window in the heavy door to make sure the boy was fast asleep. Then he pulled out the key and put it in the door.

The boy sat up in bed immediately as the man entered, and he had to hurry to shut it behind him and close it safely. Then he turned and grinned, but the boy couldn't see that, since his face was covered by the ski mask.

"What are you doing here?" the boy said and jumped out of bed. He lifted his hands to show he was prepared to fight. The man chuckled and shook his head. They were all so alike.

This boy was also a rapist. A lot of them were. According to his papers, he was seventeen-years-old, and he raped three women, all single mothers, by breaking in to their apartments while they were sleeping and put a hand over their mouths, threatening to kill their children if they screamed or resisted. This boy was really bad, he thought to himself, as he watched him. He really needed to be stopped. Doing time didn't seem to help anything. This was his second time in prison, yet he had still done it again. If someone didn't intervene, this boy would end up raping and maybe even killing more women as soon as he was released. In two months, he was up for probation. It was time for action.

The boy was dancing like a boxer, throwing punches at the man, but the man moved too fast and none of them hit. He decided to play along with his little game. Soon the man saw an opening and threw in a punch that knocked the boy backwards and into the wall. The air was knocked out of him immediately, and the man was able to grab him, put his hand over his mouth, and throw him on the bed. He saw the anxiety in the boy's eyes and smelled his fear, breathed it in. The boy knew he was in trouble. Nothing before this moment had ever frightened him before; the man knew that much. They all shared the same story. The Danish prison system simply wasn't punishment enough for these young boys. Yes, they were detainees, but their life on the inside was often even better than on the outside. They got to work out all day, play pool in the living room, or hang out with the other criminals doing drugs that the guards were paid off not to notice. The government had changed the prisons the last few years to make them "more like the life on the outside," which the man found difficult to comprehend. Why should the inmates have a life much like on the outside when they were, in fact, *not* on the outside, when they were being punished for doing wrong on the outside? He didn't understand, but the prison had to obey and they had put up small shops where the inmates could buy their own food if they wanted, and a kitchen where they could prepare their own meals, or they could buy food in the cafeteria with the money the state provided them with while they were inside, which most of them preferred. Once they had done a quarter of their time, they were even allowed to go out on the weekends. Now they all wondered why this country had so much crime, why so many young men chose a life of crime.

The man had been on vacations that were more of a punishment. He shook his head as he stared into the eyes of the boy. Then he leaned down.

He felt the boy struggle underneath him, but the man was bigger than him and much stronger. He held him like that for a while. He wanted to let him feel the way his victims had felt. He had read about the Muslim countries and how they punished their criminals and found that to be very fair. If you stole something, they cut off your hand. It made sense, the man thought, while holding the boy down with one hand and pulling off his underwear with the other.

"I want you to remember this for the rest of your life," the man whispered, as he turned him around and entered him from behind, giving him the lesson he should have had many years ago.

The boy soon gave up resisting and lay on the pillow with his head pressed down, crying, while the man had his way with him.

When he was done, he turned him around once again, and then punched his fist in his face, knocking him out. Then he opened his briefcase and took out a syringe, found a vein, and injected the contents. The boy regained consciousness just as the liquid entered his body and then stared at the man, shivering in fear. The man stroked his cheek, and then looked into his eyes again.

"Take a good look at my face and my eyes. They will be the last thing you ever see. This way you'll never lust after another woman again."

The boy struggled again, but soon the anesthesia kicked in and his body went numb. Only his eyes were open, when the man poured in the acid.

7

ALI HAD COME BACK. Brian had seen him Sunday afternoon being helped back into his cell. Brian hadn't gone into the confessional after all, but the following night he wished he had. He wished he had talked to the priest about what was happening in the prison, about his anxiety, but he was also afraid the priest would laugh at him, the way his fellow inmates would if they knew that the nightly attacks scared him. They asked Ali who attacked him, but rumors said that he didn't know. That told Brian that he knew exactly who it was, but he was afraid of being hurt again, and therefore chose to keep quiet.

Now it was happening again. Brian heard the screams early in the morning when the sun had almost risen. This time it was across the hall. A guy named Jon, who Brian had talked to on several occasions, and even shared a joint with in the courtyard when no one saw them. His screams went right through Brian's bones, and he stormed to the small window and peeked out. Guards were walking to Jon's cell and opened the door. Brian felt a shiver go through his body as he saw one of the guards, the first one to go in, come out of the cell and throw up on the floor in the hallway. Others were covering their faces with their hands.

Brian felt his heart pounding in his chest as he heard the sound of the ambulance and watched the paramedics arrive. He kept watching till they brought out the stretcher, then he turned his head away.

At breakfast, he looked at Gunnar and Torben. "What's the word?" he said.

Gunnar growled with his mouth full. Johnny sat next to Brian in silence, listening in as well.

"His eyes," Gunnar said and pointed at his own. "Acid. Roasted them."

Brian let out a gasp that he regretted.

Johnny growled next to him. "This has happened before?"

Brian nodded. "Five times since I came here, but it seems to be getting worse."

"They have no idea who's behind it," Gunnar said. "They all say they don't know who attacked them."

"Bullshit," Johnny said.

"You think they're just afraid?" Brian said, looking at his cornflakes that he had no appetite for.

"Wouldn't you be?" Johnny said.

Brian nodded while biting his lip. He knew he would. He would be very afraid. No one knew what they would come up with next.

"Could it be those guys?" Johnny asked, and nodded in the direction of a group from the East Wing. Four Middle Eastern looking guys with lots of tattoos and big necklaces. Brian knew they controlled all the drugs in the prison; they controlled the East Wing, while Brian and his gang ran the West Wing. He earned his status by being the toughest and strongest among the inmates on the wing. He had beaten everyone who tried to take his position.

"It could very well be," Brian said.

"The guy from yesterday, the guy who lost his eyes, did he know them?" Johnny asked.

Brian shrugged. "He might have. He does sell drugs now and then. Mostly joints."

"And that other guy?" he said, and nodded in direction of Ali, who was sitting not far from them, looking like the entire world had fallen down on him. Brian imagined for a second what it would be like to live his life without a dick. He made a grimace in disgust.

"One of them is his cousin. He might have pissed them off somehow. You never know with the Muslims," Torben said.

"Ali isn't a Muslim," Brian corrected him. "His family had to flee from Iran because they were Christian."

"Whatever," Torben said.

"You think they might be moving in on your turf?" Johnny asked.

Brian shrugged. "I have had trouble with them before. Gave the big one a new nose, if you know what I mean."

Gunnar nodded, satisfied. "Brian don't look like much, but he's a good boxer. He once won the national championship. He's a fucking Danish Champion in his weight class, man."

Johnny gave Brian an impressed look. "Wouldn't have guessed."

"Well, a lot of years with shit in your life will get you angry enough to knock down anyone, if you know what I mean."

Johnny nodded. "I do. I know."

They ate in silence. Gunnar was chewing with his mouth open. Torben was mostly grunting.

"We need to find out who's behind this," Brian said, and looked over at Ali, who was eating alone, looking like every bite he swallowed was extremely painful. No one dared to sit next to him for fear of being the next victim.

Johnny nodded. "Pretty boy here is right. We need to stop them or we'll be next."

8

JOHNNY WAS SATISFIED WITH his new group. He was certain he had chosen right. These guys, especially the pretty boy, seemed smart, a lot smarter than the guys Johnny usually hung out with on the inside.

As the weeks passed, he kind of grew into the group, and they accepted him as their equal. Johnny was certain he could take out Brian, even if he was a great boxer as he claimed, but he didn't want to. He didn't want to lead the group; he wanted to be the man holding the puppet. He wanted to be the one controlling them without having to actually get himself in trouble. He had been in the game long enough to know that a guy in Brian's position was exposed and constantly at risk of being beaten or even killed. But Brian knew that as well, Johnny had noticed, and detected an uncomfortable worry in Brian. If the guys from the East Wing were the ones behind the attacks, then it was only a matter of time before they did something to Brian as well.

Johnny didn't want to see that happen, and soon he felt as protective of Brian as he had been of his younger brother for all of their lives. Johnny found himself constantly watching

Brian's back in the cafeteria or in the bathroom, well everywhere really. If anyone would stare at him in a wrong way, Johnny would grab their balls and squeeze them till they knew their place. No one spoke to Brian without going through Johnny first. The only time Johnny couldn't protect Brian was at night, and that was when all the attacks had taken place. It killed him every night when they locked the doors, and he was often awake most of the night listening to hear any screams. But for weeks, there were no more, and the group began to relax a little, thinking that maybe it was over, maybe the last two had it coming to them and that was all there was to it. But not Johnny. He kept his eyes open for anything unusual, anyone acting out of place. He knew when everyone's guards were down that they would attack, to get the most surprising effect out of it.

So when one of the big Middle Eastern guys from the East Wing one day cut in line at the cafeteria, right in front of Brian, Johnny naturally knocked him down to let him know this wasn't tolerated.

Johnny ended up being dragged away by two guards and put in isolation for two days before he was taken to the warden. It was like being eight again and in the principal's office, he thought to himself, as he looked at the warden behind the desk in front of him. The warden was a big man, looking somewhat like a bulldog. His nose had been broken several times and his face was scarred and rough. On the top shelf behind him was a row of boxing trophies.

"So, I hear you're causing trouble," he said and looked at his papers. "Johnny."

Johnny knew it was wisest not to speak, so he kept quiet.

"You think I feel sorry for you, do you?" the warden continued.

Johnny still kept quiet.

"Well, I don't. I don't feel sorry for any of you in here. This is not high school; this is not kindergarten. No one cares if you had a crappy childhood; no one cares why you did what you did. This is about punishment, and if you don't play by the rules, you'll get more punishment. You've been in isolation two days. How did you like it so far?"

Johnny stared at the warden with disdain. Being put in isolation was the worst part of prison, Johnny knew. Being alone with his own thoughts, without any distractions was pure torture to him. All he could think of was his brother.

"Well, you better get used to it, ‘cause I'm giving you two more days for what you did. You broke the guy's neck, for crying out loud. For what? Cutting in line?" The warden leaned over his desk. He seemed even bigger up close. He was grinning. There was something creepy about his eyes. They scared Johnny. It was like he enjoyed punishing Johnny; he liked to see him in pain.

"Here's the deal. If you don't learn how things work in here, we have ways of making you understand, of forcing you to never do anything wrong again. Do you know how they punish criminals in the Muslim countries?"

Johnny swallowed hard. He knew very well what the warden was saying.

The warden leaned back in his leather chair. "Very well then. I think we understand each other."

9

TORBEN WASN'T A VERY smart guy. He had known it ever since his dad told him at the age of four.

"You're just plain stupid, boy," he said, and Torben had known that was just the way it was. This was his destiny, and from now on it was all about making the best of it. With stupidity also often comes a simplicity, which he found very comforting. Torben didn't want much out of life; he never had ambitions or dreams he wanted to fulfill, and he was pretty much always satisfied with where he was and what he had. In Torben's mind, that made life manageable, and he found it was always very easy for him to settle into a new environment and make new friends. He simply just did what they expected of him, and since he was never dissatisfied, he never complained either.

In that way, life in prison suited him well. To be honest, he enjoyed it more than life on the outside, where people constantly wanted something from him or expected him to act in a certain way, calling him stupid when he didn't live up to it. In here, behind the walls and bars on the windows, Torben felt safe. No one expected him to do anything, or to be smart in any way. He could just be himself, and that made him feel good. Sometimes he dreaded the day when he was going to be let out of this place. Torben regarded the world outside as a dangerous place and it had gotten him into a lot of trouble, simply because nobody had taken the time to explain to Torben what was right and what was wrong. His parents never bothered, since they were too busy arguing, fighting, or drinking and his teachers soon gave up on him as well and let him do his own thing during class, as long as he didn't disturb any of the other children. Torben never was good at anything, except for one thing. Torben was very, very good at adapting. He could be anything his friends wanted him to (except a very smart person like a rocket scientist or something). As long as they told him what they wanted from him, they could be sure he would do it. Torben was a loyal guy too. Always had been. Especially when his childhood friend (and best friend in the whole wide world) Troels told him to do something. Torben would do anything for Troels, since he loved it when Troels was pleased with him. So, back when they both were no more than nine years old, and Troels asked him to take an old lady's purse out of her hand and run, he did it. It didn't matter to Torben that Troels had taken all the money and put it in his pocket. He wasn't in it to gain money. What mattered to Torben was the look on Troels' face when he gave him the purse. What mattered was that he had patted him on the head and told him he was proud of him. That made it worth everything. There was nothing more important than that. So, Torben continued to do as Troels instructed, and soon it had become a daily thing to steal purses and wallets from women on the street or on the bus. Troels took all the money, but soon he started giving Torben a little bill now and then to make sure he stayed faithful to him. Sometimes Torben gave him the bill back, just to show him that he wasn't interested in the money. It didn't matter to him at all.

One day Troels had told him to go into a big house by the ocean and wake up the couple living there. Troels gave Torben a gun to hold when he woke them up.

"Tell them to take you to the ATM and withdraw ten thousand. Then tell them to sit down in the street and close their eyes while they count to one hundred...no two hundred. I'll pick you up on the scooter and then we'll drive off."

Torben hadn't even blinked. He had done as Troels told him to, but even though Troels was the smart one, and in Torben's eyes knew *everything,* he hadn't known that the house they were breaking into belonged to the Director of the entire Danish Police force. She had—of course—an alarm system on the house that immediately went off and she had—of course—a gun that she pointed at Torben as soon as she came storming down the stairs. Not knowing what to do, Torben had fired a shot, but since he had never done anything like that before, he missed and blew down a lamp instead of hitting the Director of the Police. The Director then shot Torben in the leg and arrested him. He was charged with assault and attempted murder.

But Torben didn't mind. He was happy in here where every day was the same. His only wish was that Troels could be here with him, he thought now, as he lay sleepless in his bed in the middle of the night, staring at the locked door, when suddenly a set of eyes stared in through the window and glared right at him.

For the first time since his arrival, Torben suddenly didn't feel so safe.

ꕥ 10 ꕥ

THE MAN WAS PEEKING in when he realized someone was looking back. A set of eyes was staring at him from the bed. The boy was awake, he thought to himself, and hurried up. The boy had seen him, and now there was no turning back. The man put the key in the lock and turned it.

Inside, in the cell, the boy was already out of his bed. He stormed towards the man and grabbed him around the shoulders, trying to push him out, but the man didn't move. Even though the boy pushed and pushed, he couldn't move the man one single inch. The man grinned underneath his mask and began to walk, forcing the boy's feet to slip backwards. Soon, the man had pressed the boy back into the cell, and while the boy threw punches at his face and chest, he closed the door behind him. The boy hit his fist into the man's nose, but the man didn't even bother to move like he knew how to. This boy was so puny and skinny and his punches so weak, he hardly felt them. For a sixteen-year-old he was strong, the man would give him that, but compared to the man, he was nothing. It was like a mouse trying to knock down an elephant.

The boy was panting and sweating with fear. The smell was intoxicating to the man. He reached out and grabbed the boy by the throat with only one hand, and slammed him up against the wall. The push knocked the air out of the boy and he gasped for breath. The man held his throat tight and felt almost high, thinking about the power he had in his fingers right now, the power to determine whether the boy should live or die. The man felt a shiver go through his body, a thrill of excitement, sending electric impulses of pleasure through his entire body. He looked into the eyes of the boy and drank from his fear. Now the boy felt sorry; now he would wish he had never done the things that made him end up in here.

A thief. A petty thief was all the boy was. The man knew his story very well. He had been known by the police for many years before he broke into the Director's house and tried to kill her. He had stolen cars, old lady's purses, and robbed small stores. Taken what wasn't his, stolen it from honest, hard-working people, who didn't know how to defend themselves. A guy like that was going to continue even after doing his time in here. Once released, it wouldn't be more than a couple of months before he returned. The man knew it. It was always the same. It wasn't entirely the children's fault, the man never believed that. No, he blamed the parents of these young men. They never taught them properly, probably too busy with their own messes to even care. That was why the man thought of it as his job to make sure the youngsters understood; it was his job to discipline them.

None of the kids he disciplined ever committed a crime again. Those were the hardcore facts. His methods were disputable, yes, but they had a high success rate, as high as they get. The numbers spoke for themselves. Some day, the world would have to realize that he was right; some day he was going to make them all understand that the system was wrong. Weak and wrong. That it had to be changed. That was the man's biggest goal in life, as well as stopping more people from getting hurt by these young criminals, who didn't know right from wrong.

The man pressed his fingers into the boy's throat and fought the urge to just finish him off. High from the power trip, he loosened his grip and threw the boy on the bed. The boy was coughing, struggling to breathe, struggling to get up. The man felt his heart beating faster and faster from the rush of excitement. He was breathing heavily as he watched the boy catch his breath and try to cry.

"Please..." he said. "Please don't hurt me."

The man leaned over the boy's body and whispered in his ear. "I'm sorry, but I can't grant your wish."

Then he lifted his fist and slammed it into the boy's face. Blood spurted out of his nose and onto the yellow wall behind him. Then he threw a series of punches into the boy's face, breathing excitedly at the sound of the nose and the jaw breaking.

The boy was still conscious, but only barely, when the man pulled up the briefcase and opened it. This time he went for the pliers. The boy writhed and tossed when he felt the man grab his hand. The man was breathing heavily while he stuffed the boy's mouth with a pair of socks to drown out the screams. He wanted him to be awake while he received his punishment; he wanted him to watch as he took the pliers and cut off the fingers one by one.

II

BRIAN WOKE TO THE sound of turmoil in the hallway. Voices, steps, then more voices, upset voices, commanding voices, but no screaming. Brian jumped up from the bed and went to the door. He paused for a second and thought about not looking, but his curiosity got the better of him. What he saw caused everything inside of him to turn. All the guards were gathered across the hall, where a door to one cell was left open. Brian felt sick to his stomach, mostly in fear, but also in disgust from all the blood that was rushing out of the cell, like a red unstoppable river.

"Torben," he muttered under his breath and put his hand on the window. What had happened to him? What had those bastards done?

Tears pressed behind Brian's eyes as he hit his fist against the thick door again and again until his knuckles bled, then he sank to the floor helplessly. Torben hadn't deserved this. What had he ever done to them? To anybody? While Brian waited for hours for the door to be opened, he speculated like a madman, plotting revenge.

Gunnar was already at their table when Brian arrived for

breakfast. He wasn't hungry, so he went directly to him and sat down.

"This will not be tolerated," he said. "How is he?"

Gunnar lifted his head and stared at Brian, directly into his eyes, something he seldom did. Brian sank in the chair. He felt the lump in his throat grow; it was ready to explode. Gunnar shook his head.

"Dead?" Brian whispered with a shivering voice.

Gunnar didn't have to answer. His eyes told him everything. Brian fought the tears and clenched his fists under the table. He felt his nails penetrate the skin in his palms.

"Who? How?" he stuttered.

"Bled to death, rumors say. He was beaten badly, then had all of his fingers cut off. Bled to death in his bed." Gunnar was speaking fast, like he wanted to get it over with, as if getting the words across his lips was so painful it had to be done fast, like ripping off a Band Aid.

Brian bit his lip hard to not cry. He was breathing heavily while the anger rose. He scowled at the guys from the East Wing. They were smiling, laughing about something. Brian felt like jumping them and rearranging their faces, even killing them right here and now, but restrained himself. This was neither the time nor the place. Revenge wasn't something to rush, a quick reaction meant mistakes. It had to be planned in detail to be perfect. Perfection was Brian's trademark. He never made any mistakes, never acted prematurely or hastily. Plus, they would be prepared now; they were expecting him to strike back for this. He needed to act when they weren't anticipating it. It had to be like a lightning strike; no one saw it coming and no one was the same afterwards.

"When will Johnny be out of ISO?" Brian asked Gunnar.

Gunnar shrugged. "Rumors say he got a couple of days more, but you never know with Warden Damhaug. He is known to do what he damn well pleases."

"We could use Johnny now, but we'll just have to wait. Waiting is good. Gives us time to think. Think and plan."

"Damn it!" Gunnar said, and hit his fist on the table, causing the plates to rattle.

Brian stared into Gunnar's eyes and saw a vulnerability he hadn't seen before. He had cared about Torben, more than he had ever wanted to admit. Brian had too. Torben was the good one, stupid as shit, yes, but good. Wasn't a bad bone in his entire body. He just wanted to make people happy, that's all. There really wasn't much more to him than that.

"We'll get them," Brian said. "We'll get them soon enough."

12

JOHNNY COULDN'T STAND BEING in isolation. It drove him nuts, not having a TV, not being able to smoke a cigarette, but most of all the damn silence was about to make him mad. In the beginning, he had tried to keep it away by making enough noise on his own, by singing, reciting nursery rhymes that he remembered from his childhood, or even doing some basic math, addition and subtraction in his mind. Anything to keep the thoughts away, to force the solitude away. The solitude that he was so incredibly afraid of and the thoughts he was scared would drive him mad eventually if he didn't keep them out. The isolation cell was smaller than the others he had been in, nothing but a bed, a sink, and a toilet in the corner. Food was delivered through a hatch in the door, without a word, without a face behind it. Johnny soon lost time and space and, as always, slept with one eye open.

To exercise, Johnny walked back and forth in the small room, while singing some of his favorite songs. But no matter how hard he worked for it, he couldn't keep the thoughts out. They kept coming back, haunting him, forcing him to face the past he had spent so many years forgetting. When he reached the third day, Johnny gave up the fight. He let the pictures overwhelm him, and then he broke down and cried. Cried for himself, cried for his baby brother.

It was a familiar story. Two brothers growing up with a drunken father who occasionally beat up their mother. A living room packed with drunks every afternoon when they came home from school, some of them partying all night, entering the boy's rooms at night and touching them, doing things to them they knew was wrong, even though it had been going on for all of their lives. It was pretty much the same for all in a place like this, Johnny knew, that and therefore he didn't feel sorry for himself. It wasn't about what happened in the past, it was about moving on, putting the past behind him. His brother hadn't been able to do that.

Once the teenage years came and the abuse from strangers accelerated, he started doing drugs that their father provided for them, which Johnny later realized were offered in order to sedate them enough to not resist, since they were now getting stronger and harder to hold down. His younger brother lost it one day—only eleven years old—and ran to the living room, all high on something when he saw his father receive money from his drunken friends. Johnny had run after him to try and stop him from getting himself in trouble, and he saw it too. That was when they had realized that their father hadn't just been too drunk to see what was going on; it hadn't happened by accident, all those men night after night. Not only did he know about it, he was the one setting it up. He was the one selling their bodies to those awful smelling men. Angry that they had seen him, their father had run after them with a knife and cut Christian severely, and that was when Johnny had enough. He threw himself at their father and used the only tool that was always at hand—his teeth.

Now—sitting in the dark room waiting for someone to open the door like he had done so many times as a child, scared of what would enter, it brought back all those memories that Johnny hadn't wanted to think about ever since he and his brother had stormed out of the house that night and into the road while their father's screams filled the night behind them. Not even when he had to sell his body to strangers in the street for money or food, had he allowed himself to think about it or feel sorry for himself. He had done what he could to help his baby brother and keep them alive. Unfortunately, he never managed to get Christian off the drugs. When they were living in the streets of Copenhagen, pulling tricks behind the Central Station, his addiction got worse and worse, and soon he got himself into debt Johnny couldn't pay. So they stole a car and drove out of town and ended in Karrebaeksminde, where they lived in an abandoned house for months, living off the money they stole from purses and picking pockets. It was easier out there in the country; in the big city, people were more careful with their belongings. Out there in the small town, most people didn't even lock the doors to their houses, so Johnny could walk right in and look for cash or anything of value to sell. Christian got off the drugs momentarily and, for a little while, everything seemed to brighten for them, until Johnny got careless and was caught robbing a gas station and got arrested. He got four months, but when he was released, Christian had joined up with the wrong group of people. He was back on drugs and built up a new debt that he couldn't pay. He was beaten half to death one day and Johnny found him at the harbor, between stacks of trash, and had to take him to the hospital. After that, Johnny thought Christian would stay off the drugs. His parole officer helped Johnny get a job at the harbor, helping the fishermen out by shoveling fish-guts, and he was able to get them a small apartment. He got Christian a job as well, and soon he hoped his baby brother would get his act together. But Christian went out one night without a word and got high, and soon he stopped showing up at work and was fired. Johnny didn't see him for months until one day when he came to his door and told him that he had stabbed a guy and the police were after him. Johnny never got the entire story, but he gave his brother all his money and helped him steal a car. Then he told him to get the hell out of there.

"Drive all the way to Germany if you have to," he said, knowing prison would kill his brother, knowing being alone with his thoughts would drive him insane in a matter of hours.

Now, sitting on the hard bed in his small cell, Johnny could only hope—and pray—that his brother was still alive and that he himself would be after doing his time in this hellhole.

13

GUNNAR CLEANED HIMSELF UP and brushed his teeth, getting ready for bed. The doors were locked at ten. He was sad for the first time in many years. He was sad to have lost Torben, who had been his best friend ever since he arrived at the juvenile prison six months ago. Brian was a friend too, but not like Torben.

Gunnar sighed and walked back to his cell, feeling a mixture of anger and helplessness. He knew Torben didn't deserve what happened to him; he had done nothing to those guys from the East Wing, and he never did anything to bother anyone, unless someone told him to, of course. But he didn't do drugs, so he couldn't have owed them, and he didn't sell it either. No matter how hard he tried, Gunnar couldn't—for the love of God—see why it was Torben who had to be killed. Was it to scare Brian? To let him know they were coming for him? Were they just moving in on them or trying to get Brian to give over the control of the West Wing? Was there something Brian had kept from Gunnar? Had they given Brian a warning earlier, or was this the warning?

Gunnar didn't understand. But most of all, he didn't like the emotions he felt because of Torben's death. Gunnar didn't have a story like the others. He didn't have an abusive father or a drunk for mother. No, his childhood had been happy and stable, with a mom and dad who loved each other—until he turned nine.

He remembered it very well, even though he rarely thought of it anymore, simply because it made him sad and he didn't care much for feeling sad. Gunnar knew that everyone was responsible for their own happiness, and even though he never was very happy, he made sure he wasn't very sad either.

His mother had suffered from a deep depression from that horrible day and hadn't been able to snap out of it again. The *day*—when he last remembered his mother being happy, was a Saturday in April. Spring had arrived, it was Easter and Gunnar was off from school for a whole week. His parents had taken off as well, and they had rented a summer cabin on Enoe, the island outside of Karrebaeksminde, where they lived in an apartment. They didn't have much, but they had enough to be happy. Gunnar remembered his mother decided they were going to go for a walk on the beach after lunch. They were going to eat outside; even though the breeze still was chilly, with a sweater on it felt nice to sit outside and be in the sun again after months and months of darkness and playing inside. Gunnar studied a caterpillar while his mother prepared lunch for all of them. The smell of fried eggs still made him sick to this day, and he still couldn't stand the taste of rye bread. Gunnar remembered the caterpillar crawling across the tiles outside, and he picked it up and let it crawl across his hand and arm. He still sometimes felt that tickling sensation of the caterpillar crawling on him. His mother's voice telling his dad to go to the grocery store and pick up a few things, still haunted him at night in his dreams.

If he closed his eyes, Gunnar could often replay a video in his mind of his father getting into the Toyota and waving as he drove off with a big smile, making grimaces at Gunnar, making him laugh like a small child, which he, at that point, didn't feel like he was anymore, not until about half an hour later.

The sound of the tires screeching, his mother coming out, looking worried, concerned, almost panicking. Then the screaming, his mother running down the street, Gunnar running after her, yelling, "What's wrong, Mom? What's wrong?"

The sound of his own voice echoed still in Gunnar's head now when the guards yelled that the doors were closing and he was yet again locked up with his own solitude, and now his new companion, the sadness.

Gunnar threw himself on the bed and cried for the first time in many years. Cried for poor Torben, who had bled to death, cried for his dad who had been killed in a stupid car accident where a drunk driver had blasted into the side of his car and killed him instantly on that nice spring morning in April. But, most of all, he cried for himself, for having to grow up without the dad he had idolized. He cried even more for having to live through his teenage years with a depressed mother who was unable to do the simplest things, and whom he constantly tried to cheer up and be happy for, even though his heart was crushed and he felt like he was broken on the inside, even though he felt like staying in bed and crying all day too. A mother he constantly feared to find dead, feared that she would kill herself while he was in school, a mother who once told him that *she wasn't sure he was enough to live for*.

Gunnar knew why he had gotten into trouble. He knew very well why he started fighting in school, getting himself thrown out, why he hooked up with the wrong crowd and started fighting, and later was arrested for beating someone half to death. He knew why and he recognized the anger at the world for taking his dad and his family away. He just didn't know how to stop.

Right before he fell asleep on this night, he knew he didn't want to stop anymore. He wanted badly to hurt those guys and make them pay.

14

SO THE BOY HAD DIED. It was most unfortunate, yes, and not part of the man's plan. No, the plan was to save the boy from himself, as well as the innocents on the outside that he might end up hurting. No one was supposed to die.

But wasn't it so, that in all good deeds there were losses? Didn't the famous World War I French Marshal Ferdinand Foch say that it takes fifteen thousand casualties to train a major general? The man thought it was. He was also the man who said that the most powerful weapon on earth was the human soul on fire. He was so right. The man knew that very well. He was on fire; his soul was on fire for this cause. Somehow, this death would eventually turn out to not be in vain; it would eventually serve its purpose, which was to teach these youngsters a lesson. This death would scare them and make them sorry for what they did. It might even end up scaring them from doing anything bad again. No, it wasn't in vain at all. The boy had died with a purpose.

The man nodded while pointing at the doors and counting. "Eenie, meenie, miny, moe..."

The man hadn't planned on acting again this soon, but it was with this as it was with so many other things in this world. If you were thrown off the horse, you had to get back up.

The finger ended on door number seven. Gunnar Thorkildsen. The man pulled down the ski mask, remembering what he knew about this boy. A fighter. Arrested and convicted for beating a bouncer at a local club in Naestved half to death, even though the guy was twice his size. Motive? Well, the bouncer made racists remarks towards Gunnar's friend, who was from Pakistan, and refused to let him inside his club. Gunnar Thorkildsen attacked him and sent the bouncer to the hospital, where he had to have twelve stitches. He had beaten him with his bare hands. The man was impressed. He closed his eyes for a second and braced himself for the fight. This was going to be a difficult one, but the man knew how to deal with those as well. There hadn't been any to this day that he couldn't handle. This little midget wasn't an exception.

The man found the key and opened the door, careful not to make too much noise. A boy like Gunnar needed to be taken by surprise.

But as soon as the man entered, he realized that he was the one in for a surprise. Gunnar was waiting behind the door and swung his fist at the man and hit him so hard, he actually stumbled a step backwards.

Startled, he touched his jaw and felt the blood through the mask. He slammed the door shut behind him and, while anger got the best of him, he walked towards Gunnar with the stun gun in front of him.

The gun crackled in his hand and he reached out and touched Gunnar with it, leaving his body to shiver, his eyes to grow wide in shock. But, in his spasms, Gunnar's leg kicked the gun out of the man's hand and caused it to fly up into the air and land in the corner. Gunnar was fast, as fast as anyone the man had ever attacked. He sprang for the gun and grabbed it before the man could. Now Gunnar was holding it in his hand and turning it on. The blue light flickered before the man's eyes, and suddenly he felt the grip of anxiety. Gunnar grinned as he walked closer and the man stumbled towards the door. But Gunnar was faster. He blocked the door and stood with the stun gun sizzling and sparking in his hand, looking like the devil himself. The man calmed himself down, knowing he was much stronger than the boy. He walked slowly towards him, chuckling, letting him know he knew he would never use it. But he was wrong. The man was so very wrong. Gunnar stuck the stun gun right into the man's throat and held it while gritting his teeth, showing the man that he enjoyed this, that he—just as the man expected, liked to hurt people. The man felt the shock waves go through his body and soon the muscle spasms took control. The man managed to grab the boy's wrists and yank them so hard he heard the bones break. The boy screamed and dropped the stun gun to the floor, where the man picked it up. The boy was on the floor, crying in pain, staring at his hands that looked like they were backwards. His screaming was so loud; the man knew it would only be a matter of minutes before the guards heard him. Perplexed by the sudden turn of events, but yet still satisfied that he managed to somehow give the boy the punishment he so deserved, the man unlocked the door with his key, and then sneaked outside without making a sound. He breathed a sigh of relief when he heard the door lock automatically behind him.

The man was long gone before the screams finally forced the guards to leave their coffee and cake behind in the guardroom.

15

"I KNOW WHO IS behind the attacks."

It was morning and Brian had just gotten his oatmeal and sat down, when Johnny came and sat next to him. Brian was happy to see that he was finally out. He had never himself gone to ISO, as they called the isolation cell, but he knew it was tough on most people.

"Where are the others?" Johnny asked, looking around as if he expected them to be sitting somewhere else or maybe still waiting in line for their food.

"Torben is gone. Gunnar was attacked last night. Spent the night in the hospital. They broke his wrists, but otherwise, he's okay, rumors say."

"What do you mean 'gone'?" Johnny asked.

"Dead," Brian said, swallowing hard to keep the tears of fear and anxiety in place.

"Dead?"

Brian nodded. He woke in the middle of the night and recognized the screams as Gunnar's and was relieved that he, at least, was able to scream, which meant he wasn't dead. Brian hadn't slept any more that night, and as soon as their doors were opened, he found the guy he knew Gunnar usually got his information from, the guy who knew everything that went on in this place before everyone else, for the simple reason that he gave one of the guards a blowjob from time to time in exchange for information. In a place like this, information was king. So were cigarettes, by the way, which he also got for his services and sold for a cheap price to the rest of them.

He told Brian that Gunnar was in the hospital with two broken wrists. Brian paid him for his information, while feeling relieved that it wasn't worse than that, but still furious that the guys from the East Wing once again had managed to hurt him.

"Torben was killed in his cell the other night. Bled to death."

"Wow," Johnny said.

"I know. We're planning his revenge, and now Gunnar's too for what they did to him."

"You afraid you might be next?" Johnny said with his mouth full of cereal and milk.

Brian sniffled, and then spat on the floor. "I'm ready for them if they dare coming near."

"I don't think it's the East Wing guys, man," Johnny said and ate some more cereal.

Brian looked at him. "What do you mean?"

"I had a lot of time to think in ISO, and I don't think it's them."

Brian scoffed. "Who else could it be?"

"The warden, man. I tell you, he creeps me out."

Brian laughed and shook his head. "You're insane," he said.

"I don't think I am," Johnny said. "There was something he said. When I was in his office and he decided to keep me in ISO for a few more days, just for the fun of it, just to teach me a lesson."

"And what was that?"

"He talked about the Muslim countries. How they punished their criminals and then he said that they had a way here to make people understand, to make them never do wrong things again. He asked me if I knew how they punished criminals in the Muslim countries and then said something about us understanding each other."

"I don't understand," Brian said, feeling confused.

Johnny looked behind his back and then to the sides to make sure no one was listening in, and then he leaned over to Brian and spoke with a low voice:

"I think he likes to punish the inmates by doing it the 'Muslim way,' if you understand."

"Like cutting off their hands if they steal?"

"And putting acid in their eyes if they lust after women like Jon, and castrate them if they rape like Ali."

"And cut off someone's fingers if they steal like Torben," Brian continued. "And break their wrists if they fight like Gunnar."

Johnny shrugged. "You get the picture."

Brian sat back in the chair, feeling like the entire room was spinning. Could it be? Was the warden really that sick? All he knew was that the warden used to be a professional boxer, and that he was a sadistic bastard who liked to see them suffer and put them in ISO even for minor things. Yes, he was probably sick enough, Brian concluded.

"What do we do?" Brian said, feeling sick to his stomach. If this was true, then none of them were safe in their cells at night.

"We reveal him," Johnny said.

"Nobody will ever believe us if we try and tell," Brian said.

"Then we tell him we'll keep his secret if he leaves us alone."

☙ 16 ❧

GUNNAR CAME BACK LATER that afternoon with a cast on each hand. Johnny told him about their theory and was happy when Gunnar confirmed that there had been only one attacker in his cell last night, and that he seemed to be working alone. He could also confirm that the attacker had, in fact, grey eyes—like steel, and not brown eyes like the boys from the East Wing all had. Johnny was sure of his theory and determined to save himself from being the next victim.

"So exactly *how* are we supposed to reveal the warden?" Brian said, when they were sitting in the courtyard on the bench, smoking cigarettes.

"I might know something," Gunnar said and nodded towards Brian, who lifted the cigarette and helped Gunnar smoke. He inhaled and Brian withdrew the cigarette and smoked it himself. Gunnar blew out the smoke and the wind carried it across the courtyard through the air.

"Like what?" Johnny asked.

"Well, the thing is, I hurt him. I managed to get the stun gun from him and put it to his throat. It paralyzed him for a few seconds, but not enough, apparently. I thought about it in the hospital while they put the casts on my hands." Gunnar nodded towards Brian again, and the cigarette was placed between his lips.

"I didn't know this, but a stun gun actually leaves a mark," he continued. He looked at Brian. "Lift up my shirt," he said.

Brian grabbed his T-shirt on the side and lifted it. Gunnar was badly bruised, but between the purple marks was another one, one that looked completely different. It was a bunch of small holes with a red ring around them.

"The ring and the small holes. That's from the stun gun. A nurse told me that."

"So what you're saying is we need to look for a mark like that on the warden's throat?" Johnny said, and killed the cigarette under his sneakers.

"If it left a mark like this on me, it must have left at least something like it on him as well."

Brian agreed to be the one to do it. Gunnar said he would have volunteered as well, but with both hands in casts, he felt kind of handicapped. After four days in ISO Johnny, was afraid to go back. Brian said he didn't mind; he could take it if it came to that.

It wasn't often they saw the warden, but every day at four o'clock, just before he went home to his wife and kids, he would stroll through the hallways to make sure everything was in place, always flanked by at least two prison guards, who would act even more viciously towards the inmates than usual, just to show off to the warden. Often, they would yell at them and tell them to behave, even sometimes pick someone innocent and beat him with their truncheons if they felt like it. Normally, they hid from this parade, but not today. Today they were planning on being first in line as the warden walked by. This afternoon, Johnny, Brian, and Gunnar were going to be taking an extra careful look at the warden's neck.

They all stood outside Brian's cell when the clock struck four and the warden began his stroll. The guards were already talking loudly and yelling at the inmates, telling them to watch out, to go back to their cells, and not stand around doing nothing. Most of the inmates crept back inside and sat on their beds while the warden passed, strolled *like a king in his parade*, Brian thought to himself. *Like the naked Emperor who thought everyone was admiring his new clothes.*

The comparison made Brian chuckle as the warden came closer. The warden suddenly looked at him. Their eyes locked for a second and Brian was certain he detected just the right amount of viciousness he would expect from the person who had been hurting his friends. Brian stopped laughing as their eyes locked. He felt a chill of anger and breathed heavily to calm himself down, to restrain himself from throwing himself at the warden and killing him with his bare hands. He thought of Torben for a second and clenched his fists hard. The warden walked while staring into Brian's eyes. At that moment, Brian was certain the warden could feel his hatred towards him. At least he must have detected something in him, or else he wouldn't have approached him instead of just passing by.

Brian stared wildly at the warden's throat as he came closer. He was wearing a turtleneck, probably to cover up the bruises, Brian thought, and kept staring at it. Brian bit his lip to keep from saying anything.

Not yet. Not just yet. Let him come a little closer.

The warden walked even closer, now with a smirk on his face, making it even harder for Brian to restrain himself.

"And what do we have here?" the warden said. He walked up to Brian and patted him on the cheek. "Such a pretty boy," he added. "Such a shame it will go to waste in here." The warden held on to Brian's chin and then squeezed it hard, like he was angry about something. His nostrils were moving heavily, like he was excited. Brian felt a wave of disgust run through his body. The warden let go of his chin and then started laughing like a madman, turning his head to look at the guards. As he did, Brian reached up and pulled down the turtleneck.

Brian stepped backwards, startled, as the warden turned and grabbed his hand and held on to it tight, speaking through gritted teeth.

"Careful what you do, boy."

Brian stared frantically at the bare neck. *There was nothing there. There was no mark!*

Brian shook his head and felt the desperation rise on the inside. The warden was hurting his wrist. "It has to be you," Brian whispered. "I just know it's you." Not knowing what else to do, Brian clenched his fist and slammed it into the warden's face, wanting to hurt him, wanting to get the revenge he had longed for. But Brian couldn't stop. He kept hitting the warden till he fell backwards. Out of the corner of his eye, he saw the guards spring towards them in slow-motion, but before they could grab him, he managed to throw in a couple of more punches and a kick.

Then he felt a pain in the back of his head and everything went black.

17

"FORGIVE ME FATHER, for I have sinned."

Johnny chose his words carefully, imitating what he had seen in movies, which were the only place he had ever seen a confessional before. Actually, Johnny had never been to church before in his entire life, so this was all very new. But today he felt like he needed it somehow. He needed to talk to someone.

The priest behind the curtain was quiet for a second, and Johnny wondered if he had done it wrong somehow. Then he spoke.

"How can I help you, son?"

"I don't really know how to do this, but I thought I'd give it a try. So, what do I do?" Johnny asked.

"There is no right or wrong way, child. You are new here?"

"Yes."

"Is it your first time in prison?"

Johnny bit his lip. He considered lying, but then thought it kind of messed up the entire point of it all. He was here to be honest, to tell the truth to someone who would have to keep his mouth shut about it.

"No. It's my third. But this time I didn't do it."

The priest went quiet for a second.

"I guess you hear that a lot," Johnny said.

"Well, yes," the priest answered. "But we are not here to talk about others. We are here to talk about you. What did you have on your mind, child?"

Johnny drew in a deep breath. This was an unusual situation for him and he suddenly wasn't sure he was ready for it yet. He wasn't quite sure if he could trust this priest to not pass on everything he said. "This is confidential, right?"

"Yes. I'm not allowed to tell anyone what you tell me."

"Okay. That's good."

Johnny considered once again leaving and maybe trying again another day, but there was something that worried him. Something he needed to get off his chest.

"I fear I might be in danger. I fear I might get hurt," he said.

"Okay. Why is that?"

"Well there have been all these attacks on the inmates and...well, I'm afraid I might be next."

"Life is dangerous, my child; this prison isn't a safe haven for anyone."

It was a strange answer, Johnny thought, and wondered if he dared telling the priest about Brian and what happened to him. Johnny hadn't slept all night since the incident with the warden, afraid that the warden would come after him next. He had to know that they were buddies.

"I'm worried about a friend of mine," he said instead. "He's in danger," Johnny said. "He's done some stupid stuff and I'm afraid he's going to get himself killed or seriously hurt."

"So you feel like you should be protecting him, is that it?"

"Yes. But I can't..."

The priest went quiet for a little while and Johnny suddenly wondered why he had come in here at all. What did he expect the priest to be able to do? Even if he told him about the warden, he couldn't stop him.

"Do you want to talk about what you did to get two years in here?"

"No." Johnny suddenly felt an eerie feeling. How did the priest know how much time he had gotten?

"Okay. But it is your third time inside, and you're how old?" the priest asked.

"Eighteen."

"And how old is your brother?" the priest asked.

Johnny paused. What was this? Did the priest know about his brother?

"Sixteen."

"And you worry about him too?"

"He's more like a twelve-year-old, you know. Mentally, he's not very bright. He doesn't know how to take care of himself."

"What about you?" the priest asked.

Johnny shook his head. "What about me?"

"Who takes care of you? Who protects you?"

"What do you mean? I do. I take care of myself and my brother. I always have and always will."

"Is that why you lied to the police and told them you had stabbed that man, when it was really your brother?"

"What the hell are you talking about? I thought you didn't know anything about me!" Johnny said, feeling the anger rise inside of him.

"Does it matter if I know you or not?"

Johnny shrugged. "I don't know. I guess not. I'm just a little confused..."

The priest cleared his throat before he spoke. "But I do feel like it is my obligation to tell you that you committed a grave sin when you lied."

"It was to help my brother."

"Yes," the priest said. "But now your brother is out there in trouble and you can't protect him. He should be the one in here. He should be the one who was punished for his deeds."

Johnny felt infuriated. Why was the priest suddenly meddling in his affairs? This wasn't why Johnny had come to the confessional at all.

"You need to tell the police the truth," the priest continued. "God will know it if you lie. It's wrong to lie, and protecting a criminal won't make up for it. There is no excuse for lying."

"It's hardly the worst thing you can do," Johnny grumbled, but the priest no longer seemed to be listening to what he said.

"A lying tongue is one of the mortal sins, you know," he said. "It's one of the things the Lord hates, according to the Book of Proverbs. A lying tongue should be cut off. In Matthew five it says, '*so, if your eye—even your good eye—causes you to lust, gouge it out and throw it away. It is better for you to lose one part of your body than your whole body to be thrown into hell. And if your hand—even your stronger hand—causes you to sin, cut it off and throw it away.*'"

That was it, Johnny thought. "Go to Hell," he said, then got up from the chair. He wanted to leave, he really did, and that might even have saved him from what happened next. But he didn't leave. No, it was like there was something that pulled in him, a curiosity, a feeling, call it what you want, but it was something strong enough to make him grab the curtain instead and pull it aside.

The sight of the priest's grinning face wasn't what alarmed him. It was what was on his neck, behind the collar, that Johnny could only see when he moved.

"What is it, my son?" the priest asked.

IN ANOTHER WING OF THE PRISON, JOHNNY WOKE MANY

hours later. He opened his eyes, feeling his heart beat hard. He couldn't remember what had happened after he had seen the red marks and the ring surrounding them on the priest's throat. After a few seconds, he realized he was back in the isolation cell. He had a terrible headache and what felt like a swollen throat. Then an indescribable pain in his mouth rolled over him and he let out a sound he thought was a word, but it sounded nothing like he had intended it to. He couldn't seem to form the sounds properly. Then he was struck by a most terrifying thought.

My tongue, oh, good God, where is my tongue?

THE END

AFTERWORD

Thank you for purchasing *EENIE MEENIE*. I hope you enjoyed it. It takes place in the Danish town of Karrebaeksminde.

Karrebaeksminde is also the town where my horror series, the Rebekka Franck Series, takes place, beginning with the first book *One, Two...He is Coming for You*. I have put in an excerpt from the first book on the following pages.

Take care,

Willow

To be the first to hear about new releases and bargains —from Willow Rose—sign up below to be on the VIP List. (I promise not to share your email with anyone else, and I won't clutter your inbox.)

- SIGN UP TO BE ON THE VIP LIST HERE :
http://eepurl.com/wcGej

WILLOW ROSE
BLACK JACK
A JACK RYDER NOVEL
WILLOW ROSE
LITTLE BOY UNSEEN
HUMPTY DUMPTY
WILLOW ROSE
WILLOW ROSE
WILLOW ROSE
YOU CAN'T HIDE
WILLOW ROSE

BOOKS BY THE AUTHOR

MYSTERY/HORROR NOVELS:

What Hurts the Most (7TH STREET CREW #1)

You Can Run (7TH STREET CREW #2)

You Can't Hide (7TH STREET CREW #3)

Hit the Road Jack (JACK RYDER #1)

Slip Out the Back Jack (JACK RYDER #2)

The House that Jack Built (JACK RYDER #3)

Black Jack (JACK RYDER #4)

One, Two...He is Coming for You (REBEKKA FRANCK #1)

Three, Four...Better Lock your Door (REBEKKA FRANCK #2)

Five, Six...Grab Your Crucifix (REBEKKA FRANCK #3)

Seven, Eight...Gonna Stay up Late (REBEKKA FRANCK #4)

Nine, Ten...Never Sleep Again (REBEKKA FRANCK #5)

Eleven, Twelve...Dig and Delve (REBEKKA FRANCK #6)

Thirteen, Fourteen...Little Boy Unseen (REBEKKA FRANCK #7)

Edwina

To Hell in a Hand Basket

Itsy, Bitsy Spider (EMMA FROST #1)

Miss Polly had a Dolly (EMMA FROST #2)

Run, Run, as Fast as You Can (EMMA FROST #3)

Cross your Heart and Hope to Die (Emma Frost #4)

Peek-A-Boo I See You (Emma Frost #5)

Tweedledum and Tweedledee (Emma Frost #6)

Easy as One, Two, Three (Emma Frost #7)

There's No Place like Home (Emma Frost #8)

Slenderman (Emma Frost #9)

Where the Wild Roses Grow (Emma Frost #10)

Horror Short Stories:

Eenie, Meenie

Rock-A-Bye Baby

Nibble, Nibble, Crunch

Humpty, Dumpty

Chain Letter

Paranormal Romance/Suspense/Fantasy Novels:

Beyond (Afterlife #1)

Serenity (Afterlife #2)

Endurance (Afterlife #3)

Courageous (Afterlife #4)

Savage (Daughters of the Jaguar #1)

Broken (Daughters of the Jaguar #2)

Song for a Gypsy (Eye of the Crystal Ball -The Wolfboy Chronicles)

I am WOLF (The Wolfboy Chronicles)

Box Sets:

Jack Ryder Mystery Series Box Set: Vol 1-3

Rebekka Franck Series: Vol 1-3

Rebekka Franck Series: Vol 4-6

Rebekka Franck Series: Vol 1-5

Emma Frost Mystery Series: Vol 1-3

Emma Frost Mystery Series: Vol 4-6

Emma Frost Mystery Series: Vol 7-9

Emma Frost Mystery Series: Vol 1-5

Daughters of the Jaguar Box Set

The Afterlife Series: Books 1-3

Horror Stories from Denmark

The Wolfboy Chronicles: Vol 1-2

ABOUT THE AUTHOR

The Queen of Scream novels, Willow Rose, is an international best-selling author. She writes Mystery/Suspense/Horror, Paranormal Romance and Fantasy. She is inspired by authors like James Patterson, Agatha Christie, Stephen King, Anne Rice, and Isabel Allende. She lives on Florida's Space Coast with her husband and two daughters. When she is not writing or reading, you'll find her surfing and watching the dolphins play in the waves of the Atlantic Ocean. She has sold more than a million books.

Connect with Willow online:

willow-rose.net
madamewillowrose@gmail.com

ONE, TWO... HE IS COMING FOR YOU

For a special sneak peek of Willow Rose's Bestselling Mystery Novel ***One, Two... He is Coming for You*** (Rebecca Franck #1), turn to the next page.

PROLOGUE

One, two...the song kept repeating in his head. Sure, he knew where it came from. It was that rhyme from the horror movies. The ones with the serial killer, that Freddy Krueger guy with a burned, disfigured face, red and dark green striped sweater, brown fedora hat, and a glove armed with razors to kill his victims in their dreams and take their souls, which would kill them in the real world. "A Nightmare on Elm Street," that was the movie's name. Yes, he knew its origin. And he had his reasons for singing that particular song in this exact moment. He knew why, and so would his future victims.

He lit a cigarette and stared out the window at a waiting bird in the bare treetop. Waiting for the sunlight to come back, just like the rest of the kingdom of Denmark at this time of the year. Waiting for spring with its explosion of colors, like a sea of promises of sunlight and a warmer wind. But still the winter had to go away. And it hadn't. The trees were still naked, the sky gray as steel, the ground wet and cold. February always seemed the longest month in the little country, though it was the shortest on the calendar. People talked about it every day as they showed up for work or school.

Every freaking day since Christmas.

Now, it wouldn't be long before the light came back. But in reality it always took months of waiting and anticipating before spring finally appeared.

The man staring out the window didn't pay much attention to the weather though. He stood with his cigarette between two fingers. To him, the time he had been waiting ages for was finally here.

He kept humming the same song, the same line. One, two, he is coming for you...The cigarette burned a hole in the parquet floor. He picked up the remains with his hands, wearing white plastic gloves, and carefully placed them in a small plastic bag that he put in his brown briefcase. He would leave no trace of being in the house where the body of another man was soon to be found.

He closed the briefcase and went into the hall, where he sat in a leather chair by the door to the main entrance.

Waiting for his victim to come home.

He glanced at himself in the mirror by the entrance door. He could see from where he was sitting how nicely he had dressed for the occasion.

He was outfitted in a blue blazer with the famous Trolle coat of arms on the chest, a little yellow emblem with a red headless lion—the traditional blazer for a student of Herlufsholm boarding school. The school was located by the Susaa River in Naestved, about eighty kilometers south of Copenhagen, the capital of Denmark. As the oldest boarding school in Denmark, the school took pride in an array of unique traditions. Some of them the world outside never would want to know about.

The blazer was now too small, so he couldn't close it, but otherwise he looked almost like he did back in 1986. He was after all, still a fairly handsome man. And unlike the majority of the guys from back then, he had kept most of his hair.

His victim had done well for himself, he noticed. No surprise in that, though, with parents who were multibillionaires. The old villa by the sea of Smaalandsfarvandet in the southern part of Zeeland was big and admirable. It could easily fit a couple of families. It was typical of his victim to have a place like this just as his holiday residence.

When he heard the Jaguar on the gravel outside, he took the glove out of the briefcase and put it on his right hand. He stretched his fingers and the metal claws followed.

He listened for voices, but didn't hear any, to his satisfaction.

His victim was alone.

⁂ I ⁂

"We're going to be too late. Do you want me to be fired on my first day?" I yelled for the third time while gazing up the stairs for my six-year-old daughter, Julie.

"Go easy on her, Rebekka. It's her first day too," argued my father.

He stood in the doorway to the living room of my childhood home, leaning on his cane. I smiled to myself. How I had missed him all these years living in the other part of the country. Now he had gotten old, and I felt like I had missed out on so much and that he had missed out on so much of our lives too. It was fifteen years since I left the town to study journalism. I had only been back a few times since, and then, of course, when Mom died five years ago. Why didn't I visit him more often, especially after he was alone? Instead, I had left it to my sister to take care of him. She lived in Naestved about fifteen minutes away.

Well there was no point in wondering now.

"You can't change the past," my dad would say. And did say

when I called him crying my heart out and asking him if Julie and I could come and stay with him for a while.

I sighed and wished I could change the past and change everything about my past. Except for one thing. One delightful little blond thing.

"I'm ready, Mom."

Her.

Julie is the love of my life. Everything I've done has been for her and her future. I sacrificed everything to give her a better life. But that meant I had to leave it all behind—her dad, our friends and neighbors, and my career with a huge salary. All for her.

"I'm ready." She ran down the stairs looking like an angel with her beautiful blond hair braided in the back.

"Yes, you are," I nodded and looked into her bright blue eyes. "Do you have everything ready for school?"

She sighed with annoyance and walked past me.

"Are you coming or not?" she asked when she reached the door.

I picked up my bag from the floor, kissed my dad on the cheek, and followed my daughter, who waited impatiently.

"After you, my dear," I said, as we left the house.

I FOUND A JOB AT A LOCAL NEWSPAPER IN Karrebaeksminde. It wasn't much of a promotion, since I used to work for one of the biggest newspapers in the country. *Jyllandsposten* was located in Aarhus, the second biggest town in Denmark. That was where we used to live.

When I had a family.

I used to be their star reporter, one of those who always got the cover stories. Moving back to my childhood town was not an easy choice, since I knew I had to give up my position as a well-known reporter. But it had to be done. I had to get away.

Now, after dropping off my daughter at her new school and smoking two cigarettes in anxiety for my daughter's first day, I found myself at my new workplace.

"YOU MUST BE REBEKKA FRANCK. WELCOME TO OUR editorial room," said a sweet elderly lady sitting at one of the two desks piled high with stacks of paper. I looked around the room and saw no one else. The room was a mess, and so was she. Her long red hair went in all directions. She had tried to tame it with a butterfly hair clip, but it didn't seem to do the job. She got up and waddled her chubby body in a flowered yellow dress over to greet me.

"I'm Sara," she said. "I'm in charge of all the personal pages. You know, the obituaries and such. People come to me if they need to put in an announcement for a reception or a fifty-year anniversary celebration. Stuff like that. That's what I do."

I nodded and looked confused at all the old newspapers in stacks on the floor.

"You probably would like to see your desk."

I nodded again and smiled kindly. "Yes, please."

"It's right over there." Sara pointed at the other desk in the room. Then she looked back at me, smiling widely. "It's just going to be the two of us."

I smiled back, a little scared of the huge possibility of going insane in the near future. I knew it was a small newspaper that covered all of Zeeland, and that this would only be the department taking care of the local news from Karrebaeksminde. But still...two people. Could that be all?

"Do you want to see the rest of your new workplace?" Sara asked and I nodded.

She took a couple of steps to the right and opened a door. "In here we have a small kitchen with a coffeemaker and the bathroom."

"Let me guess. That's it?" I tried not to sound too sarcastic. This was really a step down for me, to put it mildly.

Sara sat down and put on a set of headphones. I moved a stack of newspapers and found my chair underneath. I opened my laptop and up came a picture of Julie, me, and her dad on our trip to Sharm el-Sheikh in Egypt. We all wore goggles and big smiles. Quickly, I closed the lid of the laptop and closed my eyes.

Damn him, I thought. Damn that stupid moron.

I got up from the desk and went into the break room to grab a cup of coffee. I opened the window and lit a cigarette. For several minutes I stared down at the street. A few people rushed by. Otherwise it was a sleepy town compared to where I used to live. I thought about my husband and returning to Aarhus, but that was simply not an option for me. I had to make it here.

I drank the rest of the coffee and killed my cigarette on the bottom of the mug. Then I closed the window and stepped back into the editorial room.

I need to clean this place up, I thought, but then regretted the idea. It was simply too much work for one person for now. Maybe another day. Maybe I could persuade Sara to help me. I looked at her with the gigantic headphones on her ears. It made her face look even fatter. It was too bad that she was so overweight. She actually had a pretty face and attractive brown eyes. She looked at me and took off the headphones.

"What are you listening to?" I asked, and expected that it was a radio station or a CD of her favorite music. But it wasn't.

"It's a police scanner," she said.

I looked at her, surprised. "You have a police scanner?"

She nodded.

"I thought police everywhere in the country had shifted from traditional radio-scanners to using a digital system."

"Maybe in your big city, but down here we still use the old-fashioned ones."

"What do you use it for?"

"It is the best way to keep track of what is happening in this town. I get my best stories to tell my neighbors from this little fellow," she said, while she leaned over gave the radio a friendly tap. "We originally got this baby for journalistic purposes, in order to be there when a story breaks, like a bank has been robbed or something like that. But the past five or six years, nothing much has happened in our town, so it hasn't brought any stories to the newspaper. But I sure have a lot of fun listening to it."

She leaned over her desk with excitement in her brown eyes.

"Like the time when the mayor's wife got caught drunk in her car. That was great. Or when the police were called out to a domestic dispute between the pastor and his wife. As it turned out she had been cheating on him. Now that was awesome."

I stared at the woman in front of me and didn't know exactly what to say. Instead, I just smiled and started walking back to my desk, when she stopped me.

"Ah, yes, I forgot. We are not all alone. We do have a photographer working here too. He only comes in when there's a job for him to do. His name is Sune Johansen. He looks a little weird, but you'll learn to love him. He's from a big city too."

❦ 2 ❦

Didrik Rosenfeldt thought of a lot of things when he got out of the car and went up the stairs to his summer residence. He thought about the day he just had. The board meeting at his investment company went very well. He fired three thousand people from his windmill company early in the afternoon without even blinking. The hot young secretary gave him a blow job in his office afterwards. He thought about his annoying wife who kept calling him all afternoon. She was having a charity event this upcoming Saturday and kept bothering him with stupid details, as if she would ever be sober enough to go through with it. Didn't she know by now that he was too busy to deal with that kind of stuff? He was humming when he reached the door to the house by the sea.

A tune ran through his head, his favorite song since he was a kid. "Money makes the world go round. A mark, a yen, a buck, or a pound. That clinking clanking sound can make the world go 'round." Didrik sighed and glanced back at his shiny new silver Jaguar. Money did indeed make the world go around. And so did he.

A lot of thoughts flitted through Didrik's head when he put the key in the old hand-carved wooden door and opened it. But death was not one of them.

"You!" was his only word when his eyes met the ones belonging to a guy he remembered from school. A boy, really, as he always thought of him. The boy had the nerve to be sitting in his new leather chair—"The Egg" designed by Arne Jacobsen—and wearing his despicable grubby old blazer from the boarding school. The boy was about to make a complete fool of himself. Didrik shut the door behind him with a bang.

"What do you want"? He placed his briefcase on the floor, took off his long black coat, and hung it on a hanger in the entrance closet. He sighed and looked at the man with pity.

"So?"

ALL THE GIRLS AT HERLUFSHOLM BOARDING SCHOOL HAD whispered about the boy when he first arrived there in ninth grade. Unlike most of the rich high-society boys, including Didrik Rosenfeldt, who was both fat and red-headed, the boy was a handsome guy. He had nice brown hair and the most sparkling blue eyes. He was tall and the hard work he used to do at his dad's farm outside of Naestved had made him strong and muscular, and Didrik and his friends soon noticed that the girls liked that...a lot.

The boy wasn't rich like the rest of them. In fact, his parents had no money. But in a strange way, that made him exotic to the girls. The poor countryside boy, the handsome stranger from a different culture who might take them away from their boring rich lives. They thought he could rescue them from ending up like their rich drunk mothers. How his parents were able to afford the extremely expensive school, no one knew. Some said he was there because his mother used to do it with the headmaster, but Didrik knew that wasn't true.

This boy's family was—unlike everybody else's at the school—hardworking, earnest people. The kind who people like Didrik had no respect for whatsoever, the kind his father would exploit and then throw away. He and his type were expendable. They were workers. And that made it even more fun to pretend he would be the boy's friend.

Despite that he was younger than they were, they had from time to time accepted him as their equal in the brotherhood.

But, because of his background, he would always fall through. And they would laugh at him behind his back, even sometimes to his face. Like the time when they were skeet shooting on Kragerup Estate, and Didrik put a live cat in the catapult. Boy, they had their fun telling that story for weeks after. How the poor pretty boy had screamed, when he shot the kitty and it fell bleeding to the ground. What a wimp.

"SO, WHAT DO YOU WANT? CAN'T YOU EVEN SAY ANYTHING? Are you that afraid of me?" Didrik said arrogantly.

The pretty boy stood up from the seven-thousand-dollar chair and took a step toward him, his right hand hidden behind his back. Didrik sighed again. He was sick and tired of this game. It led nowhere and he was wasting his time. Didrik was longing to get into his living room and get a glass of the fine nine-hundred-dollar cognac he just imported from France. He was not going to let a stupid poor boy from his past get in the way of that. That was for certain. He loosened his tie and looked with aggravation at the boy in front of him.

"How did you even get in here?"

"Smashed a window in the back."

Didrik snorted. Now he would have to go through the trouble to get someone out here to fix it tonight.

"Just tell me what you want, boy."

The pretty blue eyes stared at him.

"You know exactly what I want."

Didrik sighed again. Enough with these games! Until now he had been patient with this guy. But now he was about to feel the real Rosenfeldt anger. The same anger Didrik's dad used to show when Didrik's mother brought him into his study and he would beat Didrik half to death with a fire poker. The same anger that his dad used to show the world that it was the Rosenfeldts who made the decisions. Everybody obeyed their rules because they had the money and the power.

"You're making a fool of yourself. Just get out of here before I call someone to get rid of you. I'm a very powerful man, you know. I can have you killed just by pressing a number on my phone," he said, taking out a black iPhone from his pocket.

"I know very well how powerful you and your family are. But we are far away from your thugs; and I will have killed you by the time they get here."

Didrik put the phone back in his pocket. He now sensed the boy was more serious than he first anticipated.

"Do you want to kill me? Is that it?"

"Yes."

Didrik laughed out loud. It echoed in the hall. The boy did not seem intimidated. That frightened him.

"Don't be ridiculous. You are such a fool. A complete idiot. You always were." Didrik snorted. "Look at you. You look like a homeless person in that old school blazer. Your clothes are all dirty. And when did you last shave? What happened to you?"

"You did. You and your friends. You ruined my life."

Didrik laughed again. This time not nearly as loud and confident.

"Is it that old thing you are still sobbing about?"

"How could I not be?"

"Come on. It happened twenty-five years ago. Christ, I didn't even come up with the idea." Didrik snorted again. "Pah! You wouldn't dare to kill me. Remember, I am a nobleman and you are nothing but a peasant who tried to be one of us for a little while. You can take the boy away from the farm, but you can't take the farm out of the boy. You have always been nothing but a stupid little farmer boy."

Didrik watched the boy lift his right hand, revealing a thing from his past, something he couldn't forget. With a wild expression in his eyes, he then moved the blades of the glove and took two steps in Didrik's direction with them all pointing at him. It scared the shit out of him. It had been years since he last saw the glove and thought it had been lost. But the pretty boy had found it. Now the ball was in the boy's court.

"I can give you money." Desperately, he clung to what normally saved him in troubled times. "Is it money you want? I could call my secretary right now and make a transfer."

He took out the iPhone again.

"I could give you a million. Would that be enough? Two million? You could buy yourself a nice house, maybe get some nice new clothes, and buy a new car."

The boy in front of him finally smiled, showing his beautiful bright teeth. Phew! Money had once again saved him. At least he thought. But only for a second.

"I don't want your blood money."

Didrik didn't understand. Who in the world would say no to money? "But..."

"I told you. I want you dead. I want you to suffer just as I have been for twenty-five years. I want you to be humiliated like I was."

Didrik sighed deeply. "But why now?"

"Because your time has run out."

"I don't understand."

The boy with the pretty blue eyes stepped closer and now stood face to face with Didrik. The four claws on his hand were all pointing towards Didrik's head. The boy's eyes were cold as ice, when he said the words that made everything inside Didrik Rosenfeldt shiver: "The game is over."

3

Lari Soerensen enjoyed her job as a housekeeper for the Rosenfeldt family. Not that she liked Mr. Rosenfeldt in particular, but she liked taking care of his summer residence by the sea. They barely ever used it, only for a few weeks in the summer and whenever Mr. Rosenfeldt had one of his affairs with a local waitress or his secretary. He would escape to the house in Karrebaeksminde for "a little privacy" as he called it.

But otherwise there wasn't much work in keeping the house clean, and Lari Soerensen could do it at her own pace. She would turn on the music in the living room and sing while she polished the parquet floor. She would eat of the big box of chocolate in the kitchen. She would take the money in the ashtrays and the coins lying on the shelves and put it in her pocket, knowing the family would never miss it. Sometimes she would even use the phone to call her mother in the Philippines, which normally was much too expensive for her. Her Danish husband didn't want to pay for her phone calls to her family anymore, and since he took all the money she got from cleaning people's houses, she couldn't pay for the calls herself.

It was a cold but lovely morning as she walked past the port and glanced at all the yachts that would soon be put back in the water when spring arrived. All the rich people would go sailing and drinking on their big boats.

She took in a breath of the fresh morning air. She had three houses to clean today and she would begin with Mr. Rosenfeldt's, since he probably wouldn't be there. It was only five-thirty, and the city had barely awakened. Everything was so quiet, not even a car.

She had taken a lot of time to get used to living in the little kingdom of Denmark. Being from the Philippines, she was used to a warmer climate, and people in her homeland were a lot more open and friendly than what she experienced here. Not that they were not nice to her—they were. But it was hard for her to get accustomed to the fact that people didn't speak to you if they didn't know you. If she talked to a woman in the supermarket, she would answer briefly and without looking at Lari. It wasn't impolite; it was custom. People were busy and had enough in themselves.

But once people got to know somebody, they would be very friendly. They wouldn't necessarily stop and talk if they met in the street. Often they were way too busy for that, but they would smile. And Lari would smile back, feeling accepted in the small community. If people became friends with someone, they might even invite them to dinner and would get very drunk, and then the Danes wouldn't stop talking until it was early in the morning. They would tell a lot of jokes and laugh a lot. They had a strange sense of humor that she had to get used to. They used sarcasm all the time, and she had a hard time figuring out when they actually meant what they said or when they were just joking.

But Lari liked that they laughed so much. She did too. Smiled and laughed. That's how she got by during the day, the month, the year. That's what she did when the rich white man from Denmark came to her house in the Philippines and told her mother, that he wanted to marry Lari and take her back to Denmark and pay the family a lot of money for her. That's what she did when she signed the paperwork and they were declared married, and she knew her future was saved. She smiled when she got on the plane with her ugly white husband, who wore clogs and dirty overalls. She even smiled when he showed her into the small messy house that hadn't been cleaned for ages and told her that was her new home. That her job would be to cook and clean and be available to him at any time. She was still smiling, even at the end of the day when she handed over the money that she earned from housecleaning, while her husband sat at home and was paid by the government to be unemployed. And when Mr. Rosenfeldt grabbed her and took her into his bed and had oral sex with her, she still smiled.

Yes, Lari Soerensen always smiled. And she still did today when she unlocked the door to Mr. Rosenfeldt's summer residence.

But from that moment on, she would smile no more.

❧ 4 ❧

I awoke feeling like I was lying under a strange comforter in a foreign place in an unknown city. Slowly, my memory came back to me, when I looked at my sleeping daughter in the bed next to me. When I came home from work she told me the first day of school had been a little tough. The teachers were nice, but the other kids in the class didn't want to talk to her and she had spent the day alone and made no new friends. I told her she would be fine, that it would soon be better, but inside I was hurting. This was supposed to be a fresh start for the both of us, a new beginning. I now realized it wouldn't go as smoothly as I had hoped.

My dad had prepared a nice breakfast for us when we came downstairs...coffee, toast, and eggs. Soft boiled for me and scrambled for Julie. We dove into the food.

Before mom died, he wouldn't go near the kitchen, except to eat, but things had changed since then. He's actually gotten pretty good at cooking, I thought, while secretly observing him from the table. Ever since his fall down the stairs last year, he had to use a cane, but he still managed to get around the kitchen and cook for us.

"You know, Dad, with me in the house, you could catch a break every once in a while. I could take care of you and cook for you instead."

He didn't even turn around, but just snorted at me. "I know my way around. You would only mess the place up."

Then he turned around, smiling at Julie and me, and placed a big plate of scrambled eggs on the table in front of us.

I sighed and rubbed my stomach.

"Sorry, Dad, I'm too full. Julie, go get your bag upstairs. We're leaving in five."

Julie made an annoyed sound and rushed up the stairs.

My dad looked at me seriously.

"She misses him, you know," he said, nodding his head in Julie's direction. "Isn't it about time she got to call him, and talk to him?"

I shook my head. I hated that she had told her granddad she missed her father. Since I couldn't leave my job until late in the afternoon, he had suggested he would pick her up every day and they could spend some quality grandpa-granddaughter time together, catching up on all the years they missed of each other's lives. I liked that, but I didn't care much for him meddling in my life.

"I can't have him knowing where we are."

My dad sighed. "You can't hide down here forever. If he wants to find you, he will. Whatever happened to you up there, you have to face it at some point. You can't keep running from it. It will affect your daughter too. No matter what he did, he is, after all, still her dad."

Now it was my turn to sigh. "Just not right now, okay?"

As I got up, Julie came down and dumped her bag on the floor before sitting down again and taking another serving of eggs.

Where she would put it in her skinny little body, I didn't know, but I was glad to see her eat, despite being so nervous about another day alone in the schoolyard with no one to play with.

"She must be growing," my dad said with a big smile. "That's my girl," he said, and winked at her.

I looked at the clock and decided that I too had the time to sit down for another minute. The radio played an old Danish song from my childhood. My dad started humming and tried to spin around with his cane. He almost fell, but avoided it in the last second, and we all laughed. I began to sing along too and Julie rolled her eyes at me, which made me sing even louder. The old cat stopped licking herself and stared at us from the window. She would probably be rolling her eyes too if she could.

IT WAS ONE OF THOSE BEAUTIFUL MORNINGS, BUT A FREEZING cold one too. The sun embraced everybody, promising them that soon it would triumph over the cold wind. Soon it would make the flowers come out of hiding in the ground and with its long warm arms it would make them flourish and bloom. I really enjoyed my drive along the ocean and the sandy beach. The ocean seemed angry.

I had promised headquarters to do a story today, an interview with an Italian artist, Giovanni Marco, who lived on Enoe, a small island close to Karrebaeksminde. It was connected to the mainland by a bridge. The artist had made a series of sculptures that made the public angry because of their vulgarity. The artist himself claimed that it was his way of making a statement, that art cannot be censored. He had displayed the sculptures in the county's art festival, shocking the public and making people nauseous from looking at them.

He was the same artist who once had displayed ten blenders, each with one goldfish in them in a museum of art, waiting to see if anyone in the audience would press the button and kill the fish. He loved to provoke the sleepy Danes and outrage them. At least they then took a position and cared about something. I remembered he said he wanted to wake them from their drowsy sleep walk. I was actually looking forward to this interview with this controversial man on the beautiful island.

GIOVANNI MARCO LIVED IN AN OLD WOODEN BEACH HOUSE that looked like it wouldn't survive if a big storm should hit the beach. Fortunately, big storms are rare in Denmark. We had a big one in 1999 as strong as a category one hurricane. It was still the one people remembered and talked about. It knocked down trees and electric wires. At least one tree hit a moving car and killed the driver inside. That was a tragedy. It could definitely get very windy, but the artist's house would probably stand for another hundred years.

Barefooted, he welcomed me in the driveway with a hug and a kiss on my cheek, which overwhelmed me, since I had not been happy about male physical contact lately. So I'm sure I came off stiff and probably not very friendly toward him.

He was gorgeous and he seemed to know that a little too well. I never liked men who thought too much of themselves, but this one intrigued me anyway, which made me nervous and uncomfortable in his presence.

His blue eyes stared at me while he invited me inside. It's rare for an Italian man to have blue eyes like that, I thought. Maybe he had Scandinavian genes. Maybe that's why he had escaped from sunny Italy to cold Denmark, where the sun would hide all winter. His hair was thick and brown and his skin looked very Italian. But he was tall like a Scandinavian. And muscular. I hated to admit it, but it was attractive.

Inside, I was stunned by the spectacular view from almost every room in the house: views of the raging ocean, of the wild and absorbing sea. I used to dream about living like that. Well, I used to dream about a lot of things, but dreams have a tendency to get broken over the years.

Giovanni, in a tank top and sweatpants, smiled at me and offered me a cup of organic green tea. I am more of a coffee person, but I smiled graciously and accepted. We sat for awhile on his sofa, glancing out over the big ocean.

"So, you have just returned from the big city?" he asked with an irresistible Italian accent. His Danish was good, but not as good as I expected. I had read that he had lived in the country for more than thirty years. "What made you come back?"

News of my return traveled fast in the small community, I knew that, but how it got all the way out here, I didn't know. Overwhelmed by his directness, I shook my head and said, "I missed the silence and the quiet days, I guess." It wasn't too far from the truth. There had been days in the end, when the city got to me, with all its smartass people drinking their coffee "lattes." It used to be just coffee with milk. I didn't get that. But then again, I didn't get sushi either. Even in the center of Karrebaeksminde they had a sushi restaurant now, so maybe it wasn't a big city thing.

"I miss that too when I'm away from here." Giovanni expressed his emotions widely with his arms, the way Italians did. "Especially when I go back to Milan. I get so tired in the head, you know? All those people, so busy, always in a hurry. To do what? What are they doing that is so important?"

"I wouldn't know," I said, knowing that I used to be one of those busy big-city people always rushing off to something. Rushing after a story to put on the cover. Never stopping to feel the ocean breeze or see the flowers popping up in spring. But I wasn't like that anymore. I had changed. Having to go off to cover the war for the newspaper had changed me. Being a mom changed me. But that was all history.

I began my interview with Giovanni Marco and got some pretty good statements, I thought. I began to see the article take shape in my head. But it seemed more like he wanted to talk about me instead. He kept turning the conversation to me and my past. I didn't like to talk about it, so I gently avoided answering. But he kept pressing on, looking me in the eyes, as if he could see right through me. I didn't like that, and he began to annoy me. His constant flirting with me was a little over the top. Luckily, my cell phone started ringing just as he began asking about my husband.

"I better take this," I said.

"Now? In the middle of our conversation? Now, that is what I think is wrong with this world today. All these cell phones always interrupting everything. People using them on the bus, on trains, in the doctor's waiting room, rambling about this and that, and playing games. God forbid they should ever get themselves into a real conversation. They might even risk getting to know someone outside their own little world."

He got up and looked passionately in my eyes, and I couldn't help smiling. He was indeed over the top, but it was sweet.

"Now, tell me, what could be so vital that it cannot wait until we are done?" He thrust his long Italian arms out in the air.

"It might be about my daughter," I said, and got up from the couch.

IT WASN'T ABOUT JULIE. IT WAS SARA FROM THE NEWSPAPER. She was almost hyperventilating, trying to catch her breath. She was rambling.

"Take it easy, Sara," I said, while holding a finger in my

other ear to better hear her. "Just tell me calmly what is going on."

She took a pause and caught her breath. "A dead body. The police found a dead body. I just heard it on my radio."

"So?"

"Are you kidding me? That's like the biggest story of this century down here."

I didn't get it. Normally when we received news like that at my old newspaper, they just put in a small note on page five, and that was it. If the police thought it was a murder and an investigation took place, we would make a real article about it, but still only place it on page five. And Sara didn't even know if it was considered to be a murder case or not. It was just a dead body. For all I knew, he could have died of a heart attack.

"Don't people die in this place?" I challenged.

In Aarhus, people died every week. With the gangs of immigrants fighting the rockers, people got shot and stabbed all the time. Of course, there would be a story if a dead body was found. But it wasn't like it was one of the big ones.

"He might have fallen drunk or even had a heart attack," I said, trying to close the conversation. "I'll call the police and get something for a small article when I come back, okay?"

"No, no, no. It is not okay at all. I called Sune. He is already on his way down there. You have to be there before anyone else. I got this from the police radio, remember? That means no one else in the country knows anything yet. It is what you would call a solo story."

I liked the ring of that. I might get it on the cover of the morning paper. Not bad on my second day.

"Okay, give me the address."

5

Half an hour later, I arrived at the scene. As I got near the address, I immediately knew this was no heart attack or just a drunken man. Four police cars were parked in front of the same house, two of them called in from Naestved, the biggest city nearby. I recognized a big blue van as one the forensic team from Copenhagen used.

This was big stuff.

The entrance to the house was blocked by crime tape. On the other side of the tape, policemen searched, wearing suits and gloves, writing in their notebooks, marking trace evidence, dusting for fingerprints, and marking shoeprints.

According to the radio report Sara had heard on the scanner, the victim was a white male, forty-six years old. But I already knew that when I got there. I recognized the house and knew that it could only be Didrik Rosenfeldt. The house used to belong to his parents when I was a kid. And Didrik would come down here on summer vacation from boarding school. He was my sister's age, and I remembered them hanging out together one summer. But something happened and she dumped him and never spoke of him again. He was a real asshole as far as I knew. He used to come down here and flirt with almost anything that had a pulse. He spent his time hanging out on his parents' yacht in the port, drinking with his friends from the boarding school, harassing people who were different than they and had less money. A real prick, I would call him. That probably hadn't changed a bit.

I looked around at the small crowd of neighborhood kids who had gathered in front of the house, peeking in. In the middle, a tall skinny guy stood out. He had a green Mohawk and wore a leather band with spikes around his neck, a leather jacket, and had several piercings in his eyebrows, lips, and nose. He wore black make-up on his eyes and lips. He stood out in stark contrast to this crowd of high society upper-class kids. In his hands, he held a camera that never left his eyes, constantly taking a series of pictures. As I got close to him, I noticed that he was missing two of his fingers on his right hand.

"You must be Sune," I said, when I approached him.

He didn't look down at me, just kept on taking pictures non-stop.

"Mmm..."

"I'm Rebekka Franck. Did you see anything yet?"

"Nope."

"Has the body been taken out yet?"

"Nope."

Great, I thought. Then there was a chance we could get a picture of the covered body on the way into the ambulance. That was always a good shot for an article of this kind.

"Don't you think it's weird, since the body was found at six o'clock this morning?" Sune asked me.

Now that he said it, I did. It was three in the afternoon. Weren't they in a hurry to get the body to the lab right away and find the cause of death?

"Yeah, what does that mean?"

"That the body has been hard to get out. Maybe it was lying under something or was tied to something."

I nodded. This guy knew how to use his head. Not many could do that these days without getting hurt.

"Sounds likely."

"It must at least be a messy crime scene, since it has taken them so long. There are a lot of people in there."

I nodded again. This guy had been at a crime scene before. And it probably wasn't here in Karrebaeksminde where he got that kind of experience.

"You're not from around here, are you?" I asked.

"Nope."

"Copenhagen?"

"Christiania. Have been and always will be a Christianite."

Ah, a free spirit from Christiania. Also known as "fristaden," the free-state. It was an area in Copenhagen that had around a thousand inhabitants. They lived by what they liked to call a collectivistic anarchy. Some called it a socialist anarchy. It meant that everybody living there got to take part in all the decisions. To the Christianites, as they called themselves, it meant they were different from the rest of the society and that they lived by their own rules. To the rest of the world, it meant that this was a place you could go and buy pot on the streets of Christiania, where they sold it out in the open, even though it was illegal in the rest of the country. They were a state within the state that the police didn't touch. They even had their own flag, red with three yellow dots. Today things had changed, though. The liberal government had sent in the police and tried to fight the illegal drug trade, and they wanted to remove all the houses that the Christianites had built themselves.

My guess was that Sune wasn't too thrilled about the police in general. I guessed right.

I KEPT A CLOSE EYE ON THE ACTIVITIES BEHIND THE CRIME-scene tape and soon I spotted the detective who seemed to be in charge. He came out of the house and headed towards one of the police cars, and I yelled at him.

"Excuse me. Rebekka Franck, reporter at *Zeeland Times*."

He stopped and stared at me. He then approached.

"Rebekka Franck?"

"Yes."

Surprisingly, he smiled at me.

"You don't remember me?"

I really didn't, but I wouldn't disappoint him. Besides, I really needed his comment for my article.

"Well, of course I do," I lied.

"Michael Oestergaard. You used to take dancing lessons at my aunt's dance studio. Jazz ballet."

"Miss Lejrskov's class. Michael. Oh, yes, I do remember."

I really still didn't, but I remembered my dance teacher. Michael looked to be at least eight or nine years older than me. How could I have remembered him?

"Exactly. I used to hang out there with my brother and look at all the pretty girls. So you're a big-shot reporter now? I must admit, I have been following your career. It has taken you around the world?"

"Sort of."

"And now it has brought you to Karrebaeksminde. I heard from old Miss Jensen in the tourist-information-desk down on Gl. Brovej that you had come back."

"And she was right."

That woman did a little more than informing the tourists around here.

"So you work for the newspaper down here now?"

"Yes, I do."

"And you probably want a comment for your article?"

"I would love that." I was stunned. I couldn't believe his courtesy. Normally, I wouldn't get a single word out of the police until they had a press conference, and then I would only get what all the other reporters got.

"Well, I can't say much." He lowered his voice and got closer. "But it ain't pretty, I can tell you that."

"But, what can you tell me about what happened here? Is it a murder?"

"No doubt about it. Someone broke in through the back door and killed the guy."

"Do you have any suspects?"

"No, but we might begin with his wife," he laughed. "He wasn't exactly known as one of God's better children, if you know what I mean."

"I don't, I'm sorry. So you will be questioning the wife in the near future?"

"Sure, but don't write that. That would be interfering with investigative information. You know that."

"Then please just tell me what I can write."

"Write that the victim has been identified as Didrik Rosenfeldt, CEO and owner of the world-known company Seabas Windmills, and known as a part of the famous and very wealthy Rosenfeldt family. He apparently was killed by an intruder in his summer residence; there is an ongoing investigation, and that...is it, I think."

I wrote everything he said in my notebook.

"Why hasn't the body been removed from the house yet?" I asked.

The detective sighed deeply.

"I really can't get into that."

Sune had probably been right.

"How did he die?"

The detective got an occupied look on his face.

"We don't know yet. That's for the crime lab to figure out. I am sorry, but I really have to get on with my job..."

"But surely you must have an idea?"

"We do, but we won't share it with the public, yet."

I nodded. That's what I expected. The crime scene must have been messy, just as Sune said. I spotted Sune out of the corner of my eye. He took pictures of the body as it was finally removed from the house in a body bag and transported in an ambulance.

"Who found the body?" I asked Detective Oestergaard.

"The housekeeper found him this morning, when she came to clean the house."

"At what time?"

"She called us at six."

"Can we talk to her?"

"Well, I guess I can ask her."

I had to pinch my arm. I'd never met this kind of cooperation from the police. Were they always like this or was it because he knew me? Anyway, he left me for a second and came back with a small Philippine woman with an empty look in her eyes and an expression like she had seen the devil himself and lived to tell about it. It seemed she was still in shock and I knew I had to be careful.

I greeted her with a handshake and introduced myself. The detective left us, his duty calling. I waved at Sune and signaled I wanted him to come and take her picture. He came right away.

"So, that must have been real horrible for you," I began.

"I...I just walked in, like I normally do. Normally, he isn't in the house. I didn't expect...I mean, how could I know?"

"Of course you didn't know. Can you tell me a little about what you saw?"

She didn't look at me, but stared into open air.

"He was dead. Blood everywhere. On all the floors in the living room. All over the parquet. It was like a slaughterhouse. He was shredded to pieces. Ripped apart like an animal would kill its prey. No man could have done this. Only a demon."

End of excerpt

CLICK HERE TO ORDER

GRAB YOUR COPY HERE:
https://www.amazon.com/gp/product/B004WPP8YW/

Made in the USA
Monee, IL
23 May 2021

69352451R00062